Gotcha!

Gotcha!

Shelley Hrdlitschka

ORCA BOOK PUBLISHERS

Library and Archives Canada Cataloguing in Publication

Hrdlitschka, Shelley, 1956-
Gotcha / Shelley Hrdlitschka.

ISBN 978-1-55143-737-8

I. Title.

PS8565.R44G68 2008   jC813'.54   C2008-900482-5

First published in the United States, 2008

Library of Congress Control Number: 2008921105

Summary: The grade twelve bead-snatching game called Gotcha becomes dangerous, and Katie finds herself swept away.

Orca Book Publishers gratefully acknowledges the support for its publishing programs provided by the following agencies: the Government of Canada through the Book Publishing Industry Development Program and the Canada Council for the Arts, and the Province of British Columbia through the BC Arts Council and the Book Publishing Tax Credit.

Cover image and design by Teresa Bubela
Text design by Teresa Bubela

ORCA BOOK PUBLISHERS
PO Box 5626, STN. B
VICTORIA, BC CANADA
V8R 6S4

ORCA BOOK PUBLISHERS
PO Box 468
CUSTER, WA USA
98240-0468

www.orcabook.com
Printed and bound in Canada.

11 10 09 08 • 4 3 2 1

For Cara Lee, with love, always.

Acknowledgments

Once again, this book would not have been completed without the gentle prodding from my dear friends and fellow writers Beryl Young, Kim Denman and Diane Tullson. Thank you for your wisdom and continued support.

A special thank-you to the students of Seycove Secondary School in North Vancouver, especially the grad classes of '04 and '06, for inspiring the book and sharing Gotcha (bead game) stories.

One

From: dannyo56@hotmail.com
To: kitttiekat17@hotmail.com
Subject: hi

Dear Katie,

Just a quick note to tell you I love you and miss you and hope to see you soon. I know I shouldn't have left in the middle of the night without saying goodbye, but it was a spur of the moment decision. I guess you knew that your mom and I were having some problems, and we need time apart. Please don't be mad. Things are looking up for me right now. I've had a job interview, and I have a good feeling about this one. I am going to make you proud of me, Katie.

Talk to you soon.
:D/xo
Dad

From: kittiekat17@hotmail.com
To: dannyo56@hotmail.com
Subject: Re: hi

dad, ur right how could i NOT know u were havin problems?
i'm sure all the neighbors know 2 unless they're deaf but i
AM mad!!!! u should have taken me with u! ur not the only 1
she nags 2 death u know. without u here she's got twice as
much time to rag on me. thanx a lot for that.

Katie
and where are u N E way???

From: dannyo56@hotmail.com
To: kittiekat17@hotmail.com
Subject: RE: hi

Katie,

Please don't talk about your mom that way. She's doing the
best she can. And you're pretty much an adult now, so I
know you can handle this.

Love you lots,
Dad

From: kittiekat17@hotmail.com
To: dannyo56@hotmail.com
Subject: Re: hi

ur full of it dad! im 17 not old enough 2 vote or drink (legally). if im not mature enuf 2 do those things, what makes u think im mature enuf 2 handle my parents splitting? u + mom may need time apart (thats what all divorcing parents tell their kids) but what about me? maybe i need a break from her 2! would it be ok with u if i run away in the middle of the night? would u think thats a mature way 2 handle my problems? u didnt just leave mom u left me. ur the grownup couldnt u have tried harder 2 keep r family together? i think if u loved me enuf that would have been your top priority. and u didn't tell me where u r.

From: dannyo56@hotmail.com
To: kittiekat17@hotmail.com
Subject: Re: hi

Katie,

You have it wrong. I've got stuff to sort out, and I can't do it under the watchful eye of your mom. We each have our own lives to lead. I may be living apart from you for a while, but I love you as much as ever. It won't be long before you move away to go to school or work. Does that mean we won't still be a family? We'll get through this rough patch. You'll see.

xo
Dad

From: kittiekat17@hotmail.com
To: dannyo56@hotmail.com
Subject: Re: hi

ya right.u think u've got stuff to sort out? what about me! it's hard enuf being in grade 12, w/ exams coming up + every1 asking me what im doing next year + i don't have a clue…. + now this. + i think its weird u wont tell me where u r. afraid i might drop in and find something i dont want 2 c?

take a hike.

I feel like I've been dropped smack dead center into a beehive. The hum spinning around me is alive. Closing my eyes, I will myself to suck up some of the energy, but the empty ache gnaws inside and I still feel sluggish. I return to watching the senior-grade students jockey for position on the cold, clangy bleachers, grateful for my chair at the front of the hall, facing the crowd. It's one of the perks of being on grad council.

After a quick glance at me, Warren rises from his chair beside mine and lifts a warehouse-store-sized pickle jar over his head. The glossy, multicolored beads that have been handed down to us from last year's grad class slide across the smooth inner surface. The hum in the gymnasium slowly fades away.

"Fellow grads," Warren croons in that accomplished radio-announcer voice of his. I swear it's that delivery that got him elected president in the first place. It certainly wasn't his brains. Okay, maybe he's got some charm, and he's not hard to look at, but is that any reason to elect him president?

"It's that time of year," he continues, hypnotizing an entire grade with his seductive tones, "when the graduating class of Slippery Rock High plays…" He pauses, and in that moment you can feel the hum beginning to build again. "Gotcha!"

Bedlam erupts. I'm tempted to cover my ears. The cheering, wolf whistles and stomping of boots on metal bleachers is deafening.

It's not so much that I resent Warren being president. He does an adequate job. What I resent is that by coming in second I'm slotted into the position of secretary, not vice-president. How lame is that? And aren't secretaries now called executive administrative assistants or something? Like, what year is this anyway?

"I'm sure you all know the rules of the game," Warren continues when the uproar begins to subside, "but I'll review them, just to be sure we're in sync." He taps the side of the jar. "These beads have been passed down from many years of grad classes that have come before us. Today we'll each receive one as well as a classmate's name, someone else who is playing the game. We have hemp available, or you can string your bead on your favorite chain or whatever. But you must wear it somewhere on your body from now until you're tagged."

I feel an elbow jab. I turn to Paige, one of the five grad council members-at-large, sitting next to me. Member-at-large. Another equally stupid term, and there's nothing *large* about Paige.

"We're a team, right, Katie?" she whispers. "You promise?"

I shrug and turn my attention back to Warren. Truth is, I've always liked to play games by the rules, but Paige will do anything to win.

Another elbow jab. "Katie!" Paige whispers.

"Okay already!" A little knot of worry briefly nudges aside the empty ache. I figure I'm the only person here who's not into this stupid game. We all know what has happened in past years, how things got right out of hand. That's why we're meeting at the community center and not in the school. "Gotcha" has been officially banned as a grad activity, making it that much more attractive. We've had a record number of grads signing up to play this year. I doubt any of them felt pressured to play, like I do. I tried talking the grad council into scrapping the whole thing, but they wouldn't go for it, and I knew I wouldn't get any support from the rest of the class.

"The name you'll be given today," Warren says, "is the name of your victim, the person whose bead you must capture, which you do by tagging that person. When you capture a bead successfully, you string it next to your own and take the name of that person's victim. If the person you tag already has more than one bead, you relieve that person of all of them. If you get tagged, you turn your bead or beads over to the person who tagged you and you are officially out of the game."

We all know exactly how the game is played, but we listen anyway.

"And remember," he cautions, "that you may not tag a person and take their bead while they are in the school or anywhere on the school grounds. As well, no bead can be taken from a person who is linking arms with another person who is still officially in the game." Warren pauses, probably trying to think of more rules. Not coming up with any, he asks, "Are there any questions?"

"How much cash does the winner get?" Tyson Remmer asks.

Under-the-breath comments ripple across the bleachers. Tyson is the student who needs the money least of all, and not because he has rich parents or an honest job.

"Ten dollars has been received from each of you," Warren answers, "bringing the pot to two thousand, one hundred and twenty dollars this year. That is an all-time high and should ease the burden of college tuition for someone. Or maybe it'll be a down payment on a car? Someone might even have a debt or two to pay off." He winks at no one in particular and I swear I hear the entire female half of the class draw in a breath. "And those, my friends, are the rules. The game begins in exactly," he glances at the clock on the wall, "one hour. And if there are no more questions…" He scans the faces in the bleachers. "Then come on down and get your bead!"

This is where Warren's incompetence becomes evident. Instead of organizing a proper queue, he does his stupid game-show imitation and a stampede of grade twelve students descends the bleachers and elbows and shoves to get close to "the pres" who holds out the jar of beads. I stand beside him, clutching a knitted ski toque that contains our names, each one on a folded scrap of paper. Paige holds out lengths of hemp for anyone who wants one.

I suspect that in other years, when the grad council teacher rep helped out, this whole bead/name distribution thing would be run somewhat differently, but Mrs. Barter not only refused to assist us; she wouldn't give us any advice, either.

It's chaotic, but eventually each person has a bead, a name and some have a length of hemp. Everyone but those of us on council leaves the community center in small groups. There are seven beads and seven names left.

Warren extends the jar to me first. "That went well, don't you think?" he asks.

I dip my hand in and pull out a turquoise bead. Then I draw one of the remaining pieces of folded paper from the toque. I glance at the name—force myself to keep a poker face—and shove both into my pocket. "Yeah, it went fine," I say.

"You were amazing, Warren," Paige gushes, reaching into the jar for her own bead. "Public speaking is like the scariest thing, but you make it look so easy."

Warren flashes Paige a smile. He could be the poster boy for a tooth-whitening product, and the cleft in his chin is so perfect I wonder if he's had cosmetic surgery. Paige's skin turns a flattering shade of pink.

Paige may be my best friend, but I have no doubt that if the position of class president had come down to a tie-breaking vote between Warren and me, Warren would have got her vote.

Two

"So, we need a plan," Paige says. We've come back to the school to collect our homework. Paige takes a long suck on a juice box while I select the books I need from my locker. She crumples the empty box and tosses it toward a garbage can across the hall. It misses. She doesn't bother to retrieve it.

"Mrs. Kennedy recycles those," I tell her. I can't help myself. Paige may be my best friend, but sometimes she just doesn't get it.

"Only Mrs. Kennedy would collect garbage." Paige sighs. "But stay focused, Katie. What about a plan?"

"She doesn't collect garbage." I shut my locker and slip the lock in place. "She returns them for a refund and then buys stuff for the art room. I like her fundraising ideas."

"You would." She shakes her head. "So?" she glances down the deserted hallway . "Whose name did you draw?"

"Yours."

"Get out!" For a moment she believes me. I can't help but laugh at the look on her face. "You brat!" She smacks my arm. "Seriously. Who did you get?"

"I'll never tell." I walk across the hall, scoop up the empty juice box and slide it into the pocket of my jacket.

"Then how can we help each other?" Paige whines. "Katie, you promised we'd be a team!"

I start walking down the hall without her. "Yeah, but if I tell you, you'll tell someone else, who'll tell someone else and so on until it gets to the person I've got. No one can keep a secret, especially you." And especially with the name I've drawn, I think but don't say.

"I'm crushed, Katie! I thought we were best buds." Paige catches up to me and I notice her dramatic hangdog expression.

"Cut it out, Paige. It's got nothing to do with us being friends. I just know you too well." I glance at her pouty face. "And you know you can't keep a secret."

"I can too!" Her head snaps up. "What are you talking about?"

Hmm. Which secret that she didn't keep should I remind her of? I make my decision. "Remember the butt incident?"

"What butt incident?"

Paige feigns innocence, but I know by the way she averts her eyes that she remembers only too well. I decide to rub it in. "I innocently mentioned that Matt's looked particularly good in a new pair of jeans he was wearing, and you just had to tell Mariah, who didn't think you'd mind if she told Rachel, who didn't think Mariah would mind if she told Tanysha, and Tanysha thought it would be such a big joke if she told Matt."

"Yeah, well, I said I was sorry about that, and so what if Matt knows you like his butt?"

"Paige! You're missing my point."

"The point is you like Matt, but you're too chicken to do anything about it."

"Right."

"Oh c'mon, Katie. It's like on *Survivor*. We need alliances. You know how the game works."

"I haven't been able to make eye contact with Matt since."

"Who cares? It's his butt you want to look at anyway."

"Paige!"

"Just think of what we can do with all that money."

"But only one person can win, Paige, so I don't see what good forming a team will be."

"Omigod, Katie. For someone who gets straight A's, you can be so thick. We'd split the money fifty-fifty. Duh. One thousand and sixty a piece. How cool is that? I *know* you can use the money, and I can help you win. Now, tell me who you got."

"Nope, not telling. But I will walk home with you, arms linked. Safety in numbers."

"Oh jeez," she mutters. "This is gonna be so scary."

As we pass a group of grade ten boys, I toss the empty juice box toward a recycling container that sits in a corner. I miss, and as I'm bending to pick it up, I see the boys checking Paige out. She's too busy worrying to notice, but I glare at them. They act nonchalant but make a hasty retreat when they read my face. That's another perk of being on grad council. People treat you with more respect, though I haven't really figured out why.

"What if I forget to lock my doors?" she whimpers.

"You won't."

"And what if you're busy and I have to walk home alone?" I can hear the familiar panic rising in her voice, and when she turns to me, I see her eyes beginning to bug out.

Her arm roughly links with mine, even though we're still safely on school property.

"You'll find someone else. Maybe even Warren."

Either she doesn't hear me or she chooses to ignore my attempt to distract her. "I just *have* to find out who has my name so I can protect myself."

"You'll be fine."

"I can't stand it!"

"It's just a game, Paige. Jeez."

I may be acting unconcerned, and Paige may be getting unnecessarily hysterical, but I do know what she means. It is kinda creepy, knowing you're being stalked. Knowing someone has your name. And knowing what has happened in years gone by.

"I pulled Elijah Widawski's name."

"Huh?" I glance at Paige.

"For Gotcha. That's the name I drew."

"Oh." The timer on the microwave bleats, so I remove the bag and pour the hot popcorn into a bowl. We've only made it as far as my house from the school. Paige is afraid to walk the remaining three blocks alone, so she's waiting for her mom to get home from work and pick her up, or for the cover of dark to protect her. "Who's he?"

"I haven't a clue. He must hang out in the shop classes or something. Have you got an old yearbook so I can look him up?"

"Yeah, in my room." I take the bowl of popcorn and head upstairs. "C'mon."

Paige flops onto my bed. I grab the book and sit beside her. She's studying my bookshelf. "I can't believe how organized you are, Katie. It would take me a week to find my yearbook. It could be just about anywhere in the house."

I glance back at my bookshelf. "Yep, everything's in alphabetical order by author's last name. Yearbooks are in order of years."

"You're one sick puppy."

"No, you are." I give her a shoulder check and we both flop over.

"No, you are!" she laughs, struggling to sit back up. I press my weight into her, holding her down.

"Uh-uh. You are."

"Katie, get off me!"

"Not till you admit that you're a sicker puppy than me."

"Never!"

I crunch my shoulder into hers. She's so tiny it's easy to pin her down.

"Katie!" she screams.

"Say it."

"Okay!"

"I'm waiting," I tell her.

"I'm sicker than you."

"Louder."

"Omigod!" she groans, crushed under my weight.

"Say it!"

"I'm sicker than you!" she yells.

"Good girl," I say and pull myself off her.

She slaps my shoulder. "Bully!"

I smile down on her. "Sick puppy."

We flip through the yearbook pages until we find Elijah, and then we both gape at his unfamiliar face.

"This is like *so* unfair!" Paige wails. "How can I tag him when I don't even know if he exists?"

"Don't be so dramatic, Paige. Of course he exists. And he wants to play the game. Otherwise his name wouldn't have been in the hat." That's not quite true, I realize. My name was in the hat, and I don't want to play. I wonder if anyone else felt pressured into it, like I did. I'm only playing because I am on grad council and helped organize it, so I felt I had to sign up. "You're just going to have to do some sleuthing to figure out who he is."

"Sleuthing?"

"Yeah, sleuthing."

"What the hell is sleuthing?"

"Detective work."

"Detective work. Great. I won't look one bit obvious hanging around the shop classes. Me. Paige Harrington. I've never even been on that floor before."

"He has to surface sometime. At least to go home. And besides, you can't tag him at school anyway."

"Yeah, but I have to figure out who he is!"

We stuff popcorn in our mouths while mulling over the existence of Elijah Widawski. "Okay, I told you who my target is," she says. "Now tell me yours."

"Oh, sort of like...I'll show you mine if you show me yours?" I smile at her.

"Sort of like," she says, smiling back. "But not quite as much fun."

"Sorry, Paige, we didn't make any deals like that."

"We didn't have to!"

"I didn't ask who yours was."

"But that's what friends do. We tell each other things."

Maybe, I think. But not when the *thing* is this particular person. "If we were playing chess, would you tell me when you were two moves away from checkmating me?"

"I don't know what checkmating is. Sounds kinky."

"Oh yeah. Very." I try not to roll my eyes.

"Then I'm sure I would."

"No you wouldn't! That's why you play games," I told her. "There are winners and losers. You compete."

"Not on *Survivor*. They form teams."

"Well *Survivor* is stupid. And they all end up betraying each other anyway. I don't know why you're comparing Gotcha to that dumb show."

"Because that's what you have to do," Paige insists. "I talked to grads from last year. You have to protect your friends."

"Then the game would never end."

"Well, it always has in the past. One way or another."

It turns out Paige's mom is working late, so she has to walk home after all. She phones me after supper.

"I made it," she says. "If you care to know."

"I didn't doubt you would." I can just picture her, slinking from one dark patch of road to the next. Streetlights would be her greatest hazard. "It's not like the person with your name will already have figured out your habits."

"Oh yeah? Mariah called my cell when I was coming home, and she said Minas has been tagged by Jelani already. And then Jelani got tagged by Tyson, so now he has three beads."

"No way!"

"Yes way!"

"Huh." I have trouble getting my head around that.

"And guess what else?" she asks, clearly worked up.

"What?"

"Mariah asked Tanysha to swap names with her."

"She did? Why?"

"Because Tanysha has Chad's name, and you know what that means."

"I do?" It's like the circuitry in my brain has malfunctioned. "Chad's not going to like Mariah if she gets his bead."

"That's not how Mariah sees it. She wants an excuse to stalk him."

Omigod. What next? "This game is sick."

"Tell me about it," she says with a dramatic sigh, but somehow I don't believe she thinks the game is sick at all. She's loving every minute of it.

Maybe she's sick too.

"I wonder if Warren has my name," Paige considers. "Or Justin. They could be stalking me...now that's an interesting concept."

It's confirmed. I know she's sick.

"I made it to the bank and back without being tagged," I tell her.

"You what?"

"I had to deposit the money."

"What money?"

"The Gotcha money." Grad council secretary also acts as treasurer for some reason.

"I thought the school took care of the banking."

"It used to, but now that Gotcha's been banned, they won't do it. It creeped me out having so much money at home, so when my mom got home I borrowed the car and stuck it in my account."

She thinks about that. "You better be careful you don't spend it by accident."

"Are you kidding? I'm going to Hawaii with that money. Screw the game. Wanna come?"

"Oh sure." Her tone has changed and I can picture the evil glint in her eyes. "But let's make it Brazil. I hear the guys are much hotter there."

"Okay. I hear the beaches are nice there too."

"Who cares about the beaches?" She laughs at herself, but suddenly realizes what I've done. "Katie, you were stupid to go out alone! You could have been tagged."

"No big deal."

She sighs at my lack of enthusiasm. "It is too a big deal. Get with the game."

"Whatever."

"We'll walk to school tomorrow? Same time? I'll get my mom to drop me off."

"Yep, see you then." As I hang up, I picture Paige at home, checking and double-checking the locks on her doors. Visions of last year's incident are still fresh in her mind. I decide to check our locks too.

The feeling of being swept up by a swarm of bees has intensified. Now the whole school is buzzing with news of the game. Gotcha is only played by the grads, but the excitement permeates all the grades. Before the tone for the first period has even sounded, everyone knows who's still in and who's out. Those who are out are assisting their friends with bead-snatching strategies or starting rumors about who is stalking who. There's even name trading going on, which is against the rules, but who are you going to tell?

Paige slides into the seat next to me in English. Mr. Bell hasn't arrived yet, and Tyson is straddling his desk, fingering the string of beads he's acquired in less than twenty-four hours. A small circle of girls surround him, and he's clearly soaking up the attention.

"I think I know who Elijah is," Paige whispers over the noise.

"Oh yeah, who?"

She glances around to make sure no one is eavesdropping. "He's in the gifted program. A brain."

"Ahhh. So *that's* why you don't know him."

She swats my arm. "You don't know him either!"

Mr. Bell strides into the classroom and claps his hands for attention. "Okay, everyone, take your seats." He leans against his desk, arms folded across his chest, waiting. It takes a lot longer than usual for everyone to settle. It's that Gotcha energy. When the chatter has dimmed, he observes, "The banning of Gotcha clearly didn't have the desired affect." He nods. "Somehow I didn't think it would."

"It's a grade twelve tradition, Mr. Bell," Tyson blurts out. "You can't break tradition."

Mr. Bell thinks about that for a moment. "That's an interesting statement, Tyson. Why can't you?"

This is so typical of Mr. Bell. He expects us to question everything. Tyson must be even stupider than I thought to make such an idiotic comment in Bell's class.

"Well, because."

"Because?"

"Yeah, because." Tyson is clearly wracking his brain, trying to figure out why. "Because that's the way things have always been done around here."

Paige and I glance at each other. Mr. Bell gives points to students who participate in classroom discussions. I wonder how many points Tyson will be getting for these less than enlightened comebacks.

"I see. And you believe that that's a good enough reason to continue doing something, just because it's always been done that way?"

Clearly Tyson can't see where Mr. Bell is going with this. "Well, yeah. And it's fun." He smiles at what he perceives as his own cleverness and looks around to see who's on his side. A few of his buddies high-five each other. I suspect each of these guys has managed to hang on to his bead so far. Otherwise they might not be having so much "fun."

"Uh-huh. Fun." Mr. Bell clasps his hands behind his back and paces the room a couple of times. We all sit back and get comfortable. When Mr. Bell gets derailed, there's no telling when he'll get back on track. You can practically hear the collective sigh of relief, knowing that with each passing minute there's less time to get back to the study of literary elements. He stops abruptly and turns to face Tyson again.

"It wasn't that long ago that principals were allowed to use the strap on students who broke school rules."

Tyson sits up a little straighter, the stupid grin on his face fading away.

"That could be considered a tradition," Mr. Bell suggests.

"Yeah, but it wasn't *fun*." Tyson laughs half-heartedly at his own joke, but I can see Mr. Bell's point is finally dawning on him.

"And this country once had the tradition of allowing only men to vote."

"Yeah, so?" Tyson looks around for support from the high-fivers, but except for a couple of smirks, no one is making eye contact with him anymore.

"Sometimes traditions and customs need to be evaluated and assessed," Mr. Bell continues. I can hear a lecture coming on and slouch lower in my chair. "Questions need to be asked. Is this practice still a useful one for this community or society? Is the reason this tradition or custom came into being still pertinent today? Is the well-being of society served through this tradition? Would the implementation of a new practice make more sense, given the community's circumstances? Is the practice of this tradition safe for the entire community? Is it…"

"But Mr. Bell, it's just a game!" Tyson interrupts. He is clearly exasperated and no longer enjoying himself. "It's not the same thing as voting or strapping."

Mr. Bell considers this. "Maybe not, Tyson. But we're all aware that this so-called game has been known to get out of hand. Historically it has taken strong leaders to implement change to worn-out traditions or laws. I had thought that this year's grad class had one of those kinds of leaders." He looks directly at me. "I guess I was wrong."

That wakes me up. I feel everyone's attention shift to me. Is Mr. Bell implying what I think he is? Does he mean that if something goes wrong this year he'd consider me responsible?

I crack open my textbook. "I think we need to get back to the lesson on point of view," I say.

I can feel Mr. Bell regarding me, and then I hear him walk over to his desk. "Clever, Katie. Okay, everyone, turn to page one hundred and eight in your textbooks, please."

Three

"**M**om, I told you! Keep the door locked at all times." I turn the deadbolt and latch the chain. "And don't invite anyone in. Even if I know them. Even if they claim they're here to do homework. Even if they say I invited them. Just shut the door and call me."

"And I told *you*, Katie, I've heard that the game is trouble. I won't shut the door on people, so don't bring it up again." She's sitting at the kitchen table, her feet elevated and hooked on the rungs of another chair. Her hair is a frizzy halo around her head. She takes a big slurp of her tea, leans back and closes her eyes. I don't know why she doesn't go right to bed. This napping in the chair routine drives me nuts. She says she's just resting her eyes for a minute, but the minutes tend to run together until we're talking hours.

"Fine then." I sneak a peek between two slats in the blinds. No sign of any lurkers. "Pretend it has nothing to do with the game. It's just good sense to keep the house locked. Especially with Dad gone." Maybe that will get a rise out of her. It's like she hasn't noticed that he doesn't come home anymore. Isn't she supposed to reassure me that they're just "taking a break"?

She answers, but without opening her eyes. "Like we have anything worth stealing."

Mom works at a dry cleaner's. You'd think with all the heavy work and the heat and the sweating she does she'd be as thin as a chopstick. Uh-uh. It's a mystery to me how she can maneuver her bulk between the machines and the racks of clothes.

I finish my math homework and snap my textbook shut. The noise makes my mom start, and she snorts in her sleep, but she doesn't wake up. I don't know how she can sleep sitting up like that. Her mouth is gaping, and a thin line of drool is meandering down her jaw. No wonder Dad hasn't come back.

Placing a pot of water on the stove, I turn on the element and open a can of spaghetti sauce. While I'm waiting for the water to boil, I check my e-mail.

From: dannyo56@hotmail.com
To: kittiekat17@hotmail.com
Subject: How are you?

Your mom's okay? And how's school?

It turns out the job I wanted (and thought I had) requires you to train for 6 weeks at your own expense and I can't afford that. It's back to square one for me, but I know something will come up soon.

I sure miss you. All my love,
Dad

From: kittiekat17@hotmail.com
To: dannyo56@hotmail.com
Subject: Re: How are you?

im sorry bout the job dad. y does bad luck seem 2 follow u everywhere? i still dont understand what happened 2 yur last job. i know it was boring but it paid the bills + u seemed 2 get along fine w/ mom in those days. ok ill go back 2 minding my own business. mom is snoring in her chair right now while i make dinner. some things never change. the gotcha game has started @ school. everyones gettin paranoid. not me. i think its stupid that ppl get so crazy over a silly game. i wish I hadnt signed on 2 play. stupid stupid.

i still dont know where u are, but I guess u have yur reasons 4 not telling me.

katie

"I've got to start thinking about a grad dress, Mom. There's only three months left."

I watch as she presses her fork into the spoon and twirls the noodles around the prongs. She hasn't left the chair she had her nap in, but woke up when I slid a bowl of spaghetti under her nose. For some reason this irritates me more than ever tonight. I don't know why I'm feeling so cranky, but I think it has something to do with the chipper tone of Dad's e-mail. I've been a wreck since he left, but he sounds as cheery as ever.

"Three months seems like a long time to me."

"Not really. I've got school and exams and work. There's not that much time for shopping."

Mom is quiet for a moment, chewing her food. "I was really hoping you'd think about sewing one, Katie. I could help you."

"We don't have a sewing machine."

"We could use one at the cleaners. Ed wouldn't mind. It would be fun, a project for us to work on together."

"Omigod." I drop my fork with a clatter. "I'd feel like Cinderella or something. How pathetic."

"What do you mean by that?" she asks, puzzled, but then continues, "I don't know how I'm going to pay for the banquet, the dance, the photos and everything else. Buying a new dress just isn't an option."

"Just to jog your memory, Mom, Cinderella was left at home sewing her own ball gown when everyone else had left for the party. And anyway, you won't need to worry about the banquet and the dance and the photos if I don't have a dress." I know how mean I sound, but I can't help myself.

"Don't be silly, Katie. If you don't want to make it we can find a secondhand one somewhere. After all, most of them only get worn once." She shovels an overloaded forkful of noodles into her mouth. Spaghetti sauce dribbles down her wobbly chin and I have to look away. "And don't forget, honey," she says between giant mouthfuls, "it was Cinderella who ended up with the prince." It's a valiant attempt at humor, and she looks up and smiles.

"Yeah, but that was thanks to her fairy godmother. I can't count on one of those."

"I wonder if one of last year's grads would lend you theirs?" Mom muses. "Luanne's was lovely, and you're about the same size."

"Jeez, Mom. I can't wear Luanne's. Everyone would know."

"Know what?" Her voice rises in pitch as she loses patience. "That your mom works really hard at a demanding job in order to pay the bills, and there's never anything left over? What exactly would everyone know, Katie?" Her eyes have narrowed as she waits for my answer.

"You don't remember anything about being my age, do you, Mom."

"Maybe not, but I do know that you'd look just as beautiful in a worn-one-time-only dress as you would in a new and overpriced one."

Mom begins shoveling food in at record speed. The angrier she gets, the faster she eats. I have to look away.

"Maybe you could work more shifts at the restaurant, Katie. Then you could buy your own overpriced dress."

Maybe you could eat a little slower, Mom, and nag a little less. Then you might still have a husband, and I'd have a father.

What my mom doesn't need to know is that I do have some money saved, probably even enough for a grad dress, but that money is going into my college fund.

"There aren't any more shifts, Mom. It's really slow, and besides, if I worked more, I'd have less time to study and then I wouldn't have a chance at getting those scholarships I need." There's no way I'm going to be working at a dry cleaner's when I'm forty years old. Scholarships and college are my ticket out of here.

We eat in silence.

"Dad will help me out."

That works. An unchewed noodle must have lodged itself in her throat. She starts hacking and gagging. I turn away, disgusted, but when the noise of her gasping becomes too much I fetch a glass of water. Eventually she heaves herself out of her chair and begins cleaning up. I'm rummaging through my backpack, waiting for the inevitable lecture, but it never comes. When the two pots have been washed and put away and the plates have been stacked in the dishwasher, Mom trudges heavily out of the room, but not before I see her wiping her eyes with the back of her hand. A few minutes later I hear the sound of the bath water being run.

A lecture would have been far easier to take than this shame I'm suffering for being so mean. I know it's not her fault that money's tight. I just wish it was.

Paige is waiting for me outside the restaurant when I get off work. It's Friday night, she has her mom's Volvo, and Mariah's riding shotgun. I climb in the backseat beside Tanysha.

"What's happening?" Before I've even fastened my seat belt I can tell something is up. That crazy Gotcha energy is pulsating through the car.

"I figured out where he lives." Paige backs out of the parking stall. As we pass under a streetlight, I can see the crazy glow in her eyes.

"Who? Elijah?"

"Well duh."

"So? Where?"

"On Friar street. Right next to the Anglican church."

"How did you figure it out?"

"I looked it up in the phone book. Clever, huh?"

I roll my eyes. "So what are you going to do? Sit outside his house all night, waiting for him to come out? He's probably rented a good movie and is in for the evening."

"Oh no he's not."

"He's not?"

"No, he's not."

"Then where is he?" Her elusiveness is driving me crazy.

"We're on our way to get him."

"We are?"

"We are."

"C'mon, Paige! What's going on?"

Mariah turns to fill me in. "I phoned and asked him out for coffee."

"And he agreed to go?"

"He sure did."

"What dorky guy would turn down a date with Mariah?" Tanysha asks. Even in the dark I can see the smug expression on her face. Mariah gives her a scathing glance.

"A guy playing Gotcha perhaps?" I ask. "He's not stupid. In fact, I hear he's particularly smart. He's going to know exactly what's going on."

"Apparently not."

"You're serious?"

"Yep."

"So Mariah is going to bring him out to the car. He's going to hop in with all of us, totally unsuspecting. Paige is going to tag him, and that's it."

"That's it." Paige turns and glances at me.

I sit back. "Something's not right." I can't believe she's bought into this.

"Everything's right, my friend." Tanysha pats my knee. "No worries."

No worries. Right. It's Gotcha season. There's plenty to worry about.

A few minutes later we pull up to the house, which sits right beside the graveyard that belongs to the church.

Totally creepy. Mariah pulls down the sunshade and the mirror on the back lights up. She checks her reflection. "All set?" she asks Paige.

"All set," Paige says.

Mariah climbs out of the car and saunters down the driveway and up the path to the front door. Motion-detector lights have kicked into life, illuminating the entrance. We watch as she knocks at the door. She glances back at us and flashes a smile. Then she knocks again.

The door opens but we can't see who's there. Mariah appears to be in an animated conversation with someone. A figure steps out onto the front landing with her. The conversation continues, but now Mariah is taking small steps backward. The figure moves toward her. Suddenly she turns and hightails it back toward the car. The figure races after her.

"She's been set up!" squeals Paige. Tanysha screams and links her arm through mine. Mariah races toward the car, but she can't slow down to link with one of us because he's so close behind her, so she keeps on running, right through the cemetery and into the night. I feel like I'm an extra in a low-budget horror flick.

"Who was that?" shrieks Paige. "It wasn't Elijah, was it?"

"I don't think so." Tanysha is clutching my arm with both of hers. "C'mon, Paige! We've got to go help her. Step on it!"

"Not until I've got my bead," Paige says. She flings open the car door and storms toward the house.

Who is this brave person? Certainly not the scaredy-cat Paige I know. It's like Gotcha casts a weirdness spell over everyone.

The front door is still standing open. We watch as she pokes her head in the house. Then her whole body disappears inside

"Oh my God!" Tanysha wails. "She's just walked right into Elijah's house! I hope his dad doesn't have a shotgun."

My heart's banging in my chest too. I don't care about my bead, but I do care about my friends. I make a decision. There's not much hope of catching Mariah, but we might be able to save Paige. "C'mon, Tanysha. We have to go get her."

"No way!" she screams and grips my arm even tighter.

"We can't let her go in there alone. What if something happens?"

"Uh-uh," Tanysha moans, pressing her face into my shoulder. "I can't do it."

I consider my options. I could stay here with Tanysha and do nothing or follow Paige into the house. Staying put would be the wise choice, but my adrenaline is pumping so hard that I realize sitting still is simply not an option. At the very least, I figure I could drag Paige back to the car. I give Tanysha a little hug and then gently push her away from me. "Listen, I'm gonna go get her. Lock the car after I get out and you'll be just fine. If Mariah comes back, let her in."

Tanysha studies me for a moment but then does as she's told. "Be careful, Katie," she says.

"I will."

As I walk toward the front door I have a sudden moment of clarity. I am not in a movie, and these are not just lines I've been instructed to recite. This is my life. Real life. So what am I doing here? This lurking around a stranger's house late at night is totally not me. I seriously consider turning back and going home, but then I remember Paige and I'm torn. It's just a stupid game, I remind myself. A stupid game, a stupid game, a stupid game. "Go home," I tell myself, "go home, go home." But I don't. My feet keep moving forward. I don't seem to have any control over what I'm doing.

When I reach the door I knock softly. Paige's head pops back out. "Katie!" she says.

Well at least she hasn't been shot. I should leave now. *Go home go home go home.* I quickly link my arm through hers and pull her back outside. "Are you nuts?" I ask. I can hear the steady beat of rap music coming from somewhere inside the house.

"I didn't go any farther in than the front hall," she says. "I just hoped I'd run into Elijah." She tugs my arm and I find myself stepping into the hallway with her. The music instantly gets louder. We both peer intently down the dark hallway and don't hear the person who slips in the door behind us.

"Boo!"

I swear we both jump six feet, and Paige clutches onto me. She lets out a gasp as a tall figure darts around us and slips into a room to our right.

"Who the hell was that?" Paige whispers.

"I don't know and I'm not staying to find out." I yank on her arm but pause when I hear a muffled voice calling out from inside the room. "C'mon in. Join the party."

We look at each other, and then Paige steps toward the room, pulling me with her. My curiosity is stronger than my common sense. We both poke our heads into the room, which appears to be a den. Two guys are sitting side by side on a couch, arms linked, grinning like little boys who are sharing a naughty secret. There doesn't appear to be any father with a shotgun. Paige pulls me farther into the room.

"Hey, fancy meeting you here," the boy who must be Elijah says.

He looks just like his picture, the kind of person you'd pass right by and not notice because he just doesn't look like anything out of the ordinary. Medium build, probably medium height too. His hair is cut fairly short and is a nondescript brown color. No highlights. No gel. His face doesn't strike you one way or another with its clear skin and slightly large nose. T-shirt and jeans are not brand names, but neither are they geeky. I wonder if he works hard at looking so...so blend-in-able.

Sitting on the couch with him is Joel Keister. I've known Joel since first grade, but we've never been friends. I think he's now into mountain biking or something. I make eye contact with him but immediately feel such a jolt that I have to look away. My face burns. What's with that? When I finally force myself to look back again, there's only a trace of a smile on his face but his eyes are shining.

"What's happening?" I ask after we settle ourselves into a leather armchair, Paige sitting on the cushion while

I balance myself beside her on the wide arm. We're still firmly linked. I'm relieved that everything seems so normal.

"Not much," Elijah says.

"So what just happened out there?" Paige asks.

"I think Mariah just lost her bead."

"But you were supposed to go out for coffee with her," Paige says, playing dumb.

"Right." Elijah glances at Joel. "As if I couldn't see through that little setup."

I feel myself squirming. Admitting that a girl like Mariah wouldn't ask him out must feel awkward.

"But Elijah did just happen to know who had Mariah's name," Joel tells us.

"Oh," I say. "So the girls aren't the only blabbermouths."

Joel laughs. "Are you kidding?"

I look at Joel again and find myself drawn into his open, friendly face. This time I have trouble dragging my eyes away.

"I invited Jefferson over to be here when Mariah arrived," Elijah tells us. He's still grinning. "He owes me one."

"Jefferson had her name," Joel adds.

"I figured that." I smile at Joel and then turn to Elijah. "But why didn't he just reach out and tag her?"

"He wanted to play with her a little, watch her try to lure Elijah away. But she doesn't seem to have a sense of humor. When Jefferson asked her to guess who his victim was, her mouth dropped open and she bolted. I guess Jefferson underestimated how fast she could run."

"Yeah, she's fast. Must be all those years of soccer."

"But at least now I know who has my name," Elijah says. "I'll stay clear of Jefferson."

Paige and I glance at each other. Elijah thought Mariah had his name. Jefferson will claim, honestly, that he has someone else's, and Elijah will be totally confused. That's how Gotcha works.

But that reminds me. I tug at Paige's arm. "We better go find Mariah, see if she's okay."

"Jefferson will make sure she gets home okay, after he gets her bead," Joel says. "He's cool."

I nod.

Joel suddenly looks puzzled. "So, how come you guys are here?" he asks.

Paige answers quickly, probably too quickly. "We came over with Mariah, and then when we saw her run off, we came to see what happened."

Now it's Joel and Elijah's turn to exchange glances. "So, while you're here," Joel says, "why don't we swap notes. Tell each other what we know. We could become an alliance or something." He grins. "It seems to work on *Survivor*."

I smile back at Joel, liking his relaxed manner. It's helping me shake the Gotcha jitters.

"So whose name do you have, Katie?" he asks.

"Yours," I tell him.

His look of astonishment melts away when Paige laughs. "She told me the same thing," she says. "She's impossible. She won't give away anything."

"Even if we were to tell her who has her name?"

They all look at me. "Even if," I answer. I meet Joel's eyes one more time.

I call Mariah as soon as I get home. She answers after the first ring. "Are you okay?" I ask.

"Oh, hi, Katie. Yeah. I'm fine."

She doesn't sound fine. "What happened?"

"I got set up."

"Yeah, I figured that." She probably feels foolish.

"And he got my bead."

"That's too bad." I really do feel bad for her. Clearly this game is getting to me too.

"No biggie."

"No biggie?"

"Yeah, no biggie." She says it like she means it.

"Okay, who is this and where's my friend 'Riah?!"

She laughs. "Really. It's just a game."

"Seriously, who is this?"

"It's me, Katie, honest." She's laughing and I can tell she's genuinely cheered up, warming to her story. "It was so funny. He chased me all the way down to First Avenue. I managed to lose him a few times, and I might have got away, but my shoes..."

"So what was the funny part?" I ask, interrupting. I know what shoes she was wearing so I'm surprised she got as far as she did. He must have still been playing with her.

"The funny part is that he felt so bad about stealing my bead that he bought me a latte, and then he offered to give my bead back so we could do it again."

"What?"

"I'm serious. And he's kinda cute."

"Omigod. I can't believe I'm hearing this."

"He is."

"Omigod some more. Did you take the bead back?"

"No, but I said we could do it again anyway. Drink lattes I mean. He's going to call me tonight to confirm."

Oh, so now I get it. She sounded disappointed when I first called because she thought it was going to be Jefferson on the phone. It had nothing to do with her stupid bead.

"Katie, he's so sweet."

"What about Chad?"

"What about him? He's a loser."

"Mariah, you've been hot for him for months!" How can she be so fickle?

"Not anymore."

"I don't believe this."

"Then you better get believing, girl!"

"Aren't you mad that you're out of the game?"

"No, it's a relief, actually. And I'm really excited about meeting Jefferson for another latte. I better get off the phone. He's probably trying to call."

I hang up and shake my head. I've heard of friendships being ruined by Gotcha when one friend steals the other's bead, but I've never heard of this.

Maybe something good could come from the game after all.

Four

From: dannyo56@hotmail.com
To: kittiekat17@hotmail.com
Subject: bad luck

Hey Katie,

Just wanted to straighten you out on something you said in your last letter—about bad luck following me. That really isn't so! I've always considered myself to be a lucky guy. No one's life ever follows quite the path they think it will, but if you roll with the punches, you'll bounce back up.

I think Gotcha sounds like fun. School (and life) gets so serious, and you need games to add some zip to your days. What is the prize this year?

Love you,
Dad

From: kittiekat17@hotmail.com
To: dannyo56@hotmail.com
Subject: Re: bad luck

im glad u don't think yur unlucky. im still waitin 2 'bounce back up' from the night my dad left me + my mom.

the prize in gotcha is $2120.00. i could sure use that $. 4 starters i need a grad dress & neither of my parents seems about 2 help me out w/ that. maybe im the unlucky 1.

Katie

The persistent ringing of the doorbell drags me out of a dreamy sleep on Saturday morning. Despite my grogginess, the first thing I think about is Mom's refusal to shut the door on people. Bead-snatching people.

Oh no.

I throw off my blankets and leap onto the floor, completely forgetting that my schoolbag is lying there beside my bed. My foot hits the bag, which skids across the hardwood floor. My ankle rolls sideways and all my weight comes crashing down on it, hard. My shoulder hits the wall and I collapse between my bed and the wall. Shit! Pain spirals up my leg. It's broken. I just know it is. I grab the side of my bed and haul myself back onto it. Then I test my leg. I put a little weight on it, and then a little more. The pain is excruciating, but my ankle appears willing to support my weight.

I limp out of my room and then struggle awkwardly down the stairs, clutching at the banister the whole way. I have to pee, badly, but I also have to beat Mom to the door. I hop the few feet to the front hallway and see that she's nowhere in sight.

The doorbell rings again. Great. I'm balancing here on one foot, in my most pathetic, threadbare nightie. I probably have pillow-face, and after a quick pat on the head I know that my hair looks like a bird's nest. So now what? I can't answer the door. But I have to know who it is.

I hobble painfully to the kitchen, cursing myself for caring about the stupid game, and gently pull apart two slats in the blinds. My plan is to see who is on the doorstep without them noticing me. Yeah, right. They immediately see the movement of the slats, turn in unison and flash radiant smiles at me.

It's a perfect family. A mother, father, son and daughter dressed in going-to-church clothes and carrying stacks of pamphlets and briefcases filled—no doubt—with religious books. The woman gestures at me to open the door. Her smile is angelic, and every hair is combed neatly into place. I guess it wouldn't be very polite or virtuous to give her the finger, but the one thing I don't need this morning is someone telling me I'm going to burn in the fires of hell if I don't convert. I've been woken up by these people, possibly busted my ankle because of them, been scared out of my wits, and now I'm about to pee myself as well. I limp back to the door and shout, loud enough for the neighbors to hear,

"We don't want any!" Then I hobble as fast as I can to the bathroom.

"Who was at the door?" Mom asks, shuffling into the kitchen.

I'm sitting at the table flipping, through some newspapers that were left lying there. My foot is propped on another chair, and a bag of frozen peas is wrapped around my ankle. "I don't know. I didn't answer it."

"But I heard you yelling at someone. That's what woke me up." She begins grinding coffee beans.

"It was just some religious freaks. I told them where to go."

"Katie! You didn't!" She's staring at me, not sure whether I'm kidding or not.

"I did."

Her expression can only be described as aghast. "But I've taught you to be respectful of all people, no matter what."

"Well it wasn't very *respectful* of them to wake me up and make me trip and break my ankle and get scared out of my wits…all on the morning I could have slept in!"

"You broke your ankle?" She takes a closer look at me and sees the propped-up foot. "What happened?"

"I tripped."

She's moved around the table and is removing the peas to check it out. "Oh dear, it *is* swelling."

"See? Maybe next time you'll believe me instead of siding with the strangers at the door."

Mom sighs. "I wasn't taking sides, Katie. Why do you always have to be so difficult?" She replaces the peas. "It's just that I've raised you better than that. Everyone deserves to be treated politely."

"Really. And is that how you were treating Dad—politely—when you were yelling at him in the middle of the night?"

I've shocked myself. I had no clue, absolutely no idea, that those words were going to come tumbling out of my mouth. But they did, and now they hang in the air between us.

Mom looks at me, surprised, and quickly looks away. "There's stuff you don't understand, Katie, problems that your dad has…"

"Yeah, well, you have problems too. And so do I."

Mom sighs again. She's been doing a lot of that lately. "That's true, Katie, and the problem we have to deal with right now is your ankle. That's the most important thing." She seems relieved to direct her thoughts to something besides my dad. "C'mon, I'll help you onto the couch where you'll be more comfortable."

I put my arm around her shoulder and allow her to take some of my weight as I move over to the couch. She places a pillow under my ankle, elevating it, and puts the peas back on top. She drapes a blanket around my shoulders and hands me the TV remote controller.

"Is there anything I can get you, honey?"

"Just a new ankle."

She smiles, sadly. "Sorry. I can't do that. But I'll go get dressed, make us some breakfast, and then I'll take you to the clinic to have that foot looked at. You just keep it still."

I scrunch down, totally ticked.

Stupid Gotcha game.

Mom takes me to the clinic, and after putting my ankle through some painful movements, the doctor declares that it's "just sprained." Two hours later, with a pair of rented crutches at my side, I'm back on the couch, still fuming. I've been told not to put any weight on my foot for the first few days, and then only gradually can I begin to use it again. That means no work, and that adds up to a lot of college money.

And what about the Gotcha game? I'm a sitting duck.

The doorbell rings around noon. I begin to jump up but quickly remember my predicament. "Mom!" I holler into the kitchen. "Don't you dare let anyone in until you check with me!"

I listen as she trudges to the front hall. I guess she's taken some pity on me, because I hear the deadbolt unlock, but I can tell she's left the chain latched as she opens the door.

"Hi, Paige," I hear her say. Then, "Katie, can I let Paige in?" she yells down the hall, humoring me.

"Is she alone?" I holler back.

"Are you alone?" she asks Paige, loudly, for my benefit. "She's alone now!" she yells at me. "But her mom escorted her to the door."

A lot of good her mom would have been if Paige's stalker had been lurking in the shrubs beside our door.

"All right," I say.

Mom fills Paige in on my accident before she can even get to the living room.

"Omigod, Katie!" Paige says, seeing my now black and blue ankle. "You poor thing!"

"I'll live." I tell her. But not happily.

"Wow," she says. She plunks herself into the armchair and promptly forgets about my ankle. "So, Michelle lost her bead last night too," she tells me.

"Really?" I see the crazy Gotcha glow in her eyes.

"Yeah. It was awful. She drove to the mall alone, which was her first mistake. She parked her car and was just about to get out when suddenly Frazer appears at her window, grinning. She hits the power lock, but Frazer runs behind the car so she can't back out of the parking stall."

"I wonder why Frazer didn't just stay out of sight till she got out of her car."

"I guess he got overexcited. I don't know. But anyway, Michelle calls Christy on her cell phone and demands that she come to her rescue. You know how Michelle can be. So Christy picks up Evan, and they pull in beside Michelle in the parking lot. The plan was for Christy and Evan to link up and stand at the window. Then Michelle would roll down the window and Christy would reach in and link with Michelle before Frazer could tag her."

"So? What happened?"

"Something went wrong, and somehow Frazer was able to reach in and tag Michelle before she and Christy could get linked. I guess there was a lot of pushing and shoving going on."

"Oh-oh."

"Yeah, and now Michelle's ticked because she thinks Christy failed her. She's not talking to her."

"How stupid is that? Christy did her best. She drove all the way to the mall."

"Yeah, and Evan said it was really Michelle's fault, that she panicked and rolled the window down too soon."

"Whatever."

"And Kerry lost her bead too."

"Oh no. Busy night."

"Yeah, it was the same kind of thing. She parked in the lot outside the drugstore, and suddenly her car was boxed in on either side and behind by three other cars."

"Like some kind of police bust."

"Right. So it was just a matter of who could hold out the longest. Kerry had an early curfew—you know her dad—so she eventually just handed over her bead to Jonah."

"Huh."

"But see how it works, Katie?" Paige leans toward me, making her point. "Jonah's friends worked as a team to help him get his bead. That's what we have to do too."

I don't answer, so she carries on sharing all the news. "Tyson's having a Gotcha party tonight," she tells me.

"A Gotcha party?"

"That's what he's calling it."

"That sounds a bit random."

She shrugs. "Everyone will be standing around linked to someone else. Except those who have lost their beads."

"Yeah, they'll be the only ones having any fun."

She ignores me, but then leans forward again, looking panicky. "You'll stick with me, right, Katie?"

I decide to toy with her and ask, "What's in it for me?"

"Katie!"

I have to laugh. "Yeah, I'll stick with you, but will you stick with me? What if the Pres asks you to dance? A slow dance. Are you going to turn down *Warren* to protect me?"

"Well, duh! I could get tagged on the dance floor."

I notice she's missed my point, but I let it go. "That's true. But wouldn't it be worth it, for Warren?"

"Oh shut up, Katie! No, not even a slow dance with Warren would make me risk losing my bead."

I think about that. She really is into this game.

"So you're in?" she asks.

"It sounds like a strange kind of party, everyone standing around latched onto their best friend's arm. What's the point?"

"I think it sounds like a hoot."

"You would."

Paige decides to change the subject. "So tell me, Katie," she says, "what do you think of Joel Keister?" Her tone is taunting and she's studying me closely.

"He's okay. What do you think of him?"

"I think he's nice. But I'm not the one who was blushing when he looked at me last night."

"I wasn't blushing!"

"You were too! You were as red as a tomato."

"I was not!"

"Look at you! You're blushing again! Aha!"

Damn Paige anyway. I really can feel my face burning. I've got to throw her off.

"I've known Joel all my life," I tell her.

"You have?"

"Yeah. I think he was in my grade one class."

"Really. Then what can you tell me about him? Hmm?"

Her smugness is really irritating. "I don't know, Paige. Why are you asking me all these questions?"

"Because I think *someone* has the hots for Joel, and Joel just might have the hots for *someone*."

"Shut up, Paige! I talked to him for exactly two minutes last night. That's not quite enough time to 'get the hots' as you so eloquently put it."

"Something was clearly happening between you guys."

"You're being an idiot."

"Maybe he'll be at Tyson's tonight."

"Like I could care." But why did my heart skip a beat when she said that?

"And you never answered my question, Katie. You will stick with me, right?"

"Right. Unless someone better comes along."

"Katie!"

She's so gullible. I have to laugh. "What*ever*, Paige."

As she gets up to go, she spots my crutches and tries

them out. A worried look crosses her face. "These could be a problem for you in Gotcha you know."

"Tell me about it. We'll have to stay seated at the party tonight."

"Oh." She hesitates. "Then maybe I should have asked Tanysha to hang with me, instead of you."

I know I should bite my tongue right now. Paige doesn't realize how selfish she sounds. How selfish she *is*. On any other day I might have been able to ignore her comment, but not today. Today I have been ticked off one too many times. "Maybe you should have," I tell her. "Because how on earth will everyone be able to *appreciate* you when you're sitting in a corner with me?"

"What's that supposed to mean?" She looks sincerely puzzled, but suspicious too.

"Nothing."

"I'm serious, Katie. Don't say 'nothing.' What do you mean?"

"Okay, Paige," I tell her. Maybe it *is* time for her to know how I feel. "Listen to yourself. You come over here and beg me to go to the party so you will have someone to link with. When I hint that you might go off and leave me stranded, you only think about how vulnerable you'd be without me, not how vulnerable I'd be without you. And then, instead of giving me any sympathy about my ankle, you think instead of how my injury might affect your fun. Everyone knows you like to be the center of attention, but gosh, it might be a little hard to be that center if you're sitting off in a corner with me.

Yep, I think maybe you would be better off with Tanysha."

The words have just spewed out of my mouth, and for a moment I feel relief from the crankiness that has plagued me all morning. I'm expecting the Drama Queen to react, and I'm ready for a good fight.

But then I see the wounded expression on her face.

How I wish I could press a rewind button on my mouth and take it all back. Just as suddenly as the anger hit me, it has left me, and I remember that despite her self-centeredness, she is also fun and loveable and sweet and funny. Those things more than make up for her other qualities. I can't believe I've said those hurtful things.

My mom chooses that moment to barge in with a plate of cookies and mugs of hot chocolate. She's always believed that food can fix anything, even sprained ankles. "So, Paige," she says, oblivious to the mood in the room. "How have you been? I love your new hair color!"

Paige blinks and looks away from me. It takes her a moment to gather her thoughts. She turns to my mom. "Well, I was okay until just a few minutes ago. But Katie just finished informing me that everyone thinks I'm selfish and that I like to be the center of attention. I'm not feeling quite so okay anymore."

My mom turns to me, shocked. "Katie!"

"It's okay," Paige says to my mom. "I can handle it." She nods.

I desperately search my brain for something to say, anything to fix the damage I've caused, but my mind is blank, and I can only stare stupidly at Paige. I can see my mom looking from Paige to me and back to Paige again. She reaches out and hands a mug of hot chocolate to Paige, convinced, I'm sure, that food can even fix this mess.

Paige accepts the mug but simply places it on the table and then leaves the room.

"I'm sorry, Paige!" I holler down the hall.

I hear the front door close behind her. She hasn't arranged for anyone to pick her up, and she has no one to link arms with on her way home.

Did the truth hurt that much? Enough to take those chances?

Mom glares at me. Then, without a word, she takes Paige's hot chocolate off the table, and she too leaves the room.

Why can't I learn to keep my mouth shut like that?

Less than an hour later the doorbell is ringing again. I wish I knew how to switch the stupid thing off.

Mom and I go through the same routine. "It's Mariah and Tanysha," she calls to me. "Can I let them in?"

"Yes." I really don't have the energy for any more games today.

They both look angry when they enter the living room, but Mariah is kind enough to ask about my ankle.

"It's just sprained," I tell her.

"So why did you say those things to Paige?" Tanysha asks, getting right to the point. She looks steamed.

"Because it was the truth," I tell them. "I'd had enough. My foot hurts, I can't work…I might as well forget playing Gotcha, but all Paige cares about is her own stupid self."

I haven't told my friends about my dad's disappearing act. I don't know why, exactly. There just hasn't been a good time. And maybe I don't want to see the pity in their eyes. And the knowing glances between them. And I'm certainly not going to use that as an excuse right now.

"Paige is Paige," Tanysha tells me, as if that's news, "and she may be a little egocentric now and again, but you've really hurt her this time. She's so upset she's not even protecting herself from whoever has her name."

"I said I was sorry."

"Being sorry is not going to change what you said."

"Give me a break, Tanysha," I say, feeling my temper spiking again. "I'm the one with the sprained ankle." And the ruined life.

"An ankle probably heals faster than a crushed ego," she tells me.

This isn't the first time I've seen Tanysha come to Paige's defense. She has an unwavering loyalty to Paige that borders on hero worship. And she's not the only one. Paige has an entourage of adoring fans, and yet she seems oblivious to it. She usually singles me out for friendship, and I am the least adoring of them all. To be honest, I thought she appreciated the reality check I provided. Until today, anyway. "She'll get over it," I tell Tanysha. "You know how dramatic she can be."

I turn to Mariah, attempting to change the subject. "Did you go out for another latte with Jefferson?"

I see her face light up, but before she can reply, Tanysha grabs her arm and begins dragging her out of the living room. Mariah glances back at me apologetically, but I know she won't stand up to Tanysha or Paige. "I don't think she's going to just 'get over it,' as you say," Tanysha tells me. "You've done it this time, Katie."

Why do I get the feeling she might be happy about that?

They practically crash into my mom in the doorway. She's carrying yet another tray of snacks. She watches as they storm off, looks at me and then shakes her head. She turns and goes back to the kitchen.

Five

From: dannyo56@hotmail.com
To: kittiekat17@hotmail.com
Subject: What's up?

Hey Katie,

What's new? I'm missing you, but I'm still working at getting my life in order. Any day now!

Send me a note, tell me what's happening. (And how is your mom?)

Love and hugs,
Dad

From: kittiekat17@hotmail.com
To: dannyo56@hotmail.com
Subject: Re: What's up?

dad,
i have a badly sprained ankle. i cant work. that means im not makin the money i need 4 college or even 4 a simple grad dress. my friends hate me. ive organized a game that will probably get me kicked out of school. my father left me. my mother is a cow. i have no future. life sux.
Katie

Just when I think my day can't get any worse, the doorbell rings again. Mom stands in the doorway to the living room, hand on hip, eyebrows raised.

"Just let them in," I tell her, defeated. "I don't care anymore." I flop back on the couch and reach for the TV controller, but I put it back down when I hear a male voice at the door. My heart sinks completely. This really must be it. The only guy who would come looking for me is someone who wants my bead.

I sit up straight and mentally prepare myself. Okay, I'm ready to get it over with. They can have my bead, and my victim…I never wanted to play this stupid game in the first place…

And then Joel Keister strides into the room. Suddenly I'm not so prepared. I'm in total shock. I never imagined it would be him.

Our eyes lock, but just like last night, I have to look away. Screw him and those shining eyes. Screw him for drawing my name. Screw Paige for putting ideas in my head.

"Oh, this is just perfect," I say, hoping he can't hear the tremble in my voice. I guess Paige was right after all. There *was* something happening between Joel and me: I am Joel's victim, and he's been figuring out how to get my bead. I should have known. What else would have been happening? I am such an idiot. I blink back tears.

"What's perfect?" Joel asks. He glances from my ankle to my crutches to my face, and he actually looks concerned. No laugh lines now. Thank goodness I changed out of my godawful nightie when I went to the clinic.

"You're about to tag me." I hold out my arm. "Hurry up. Get it over with."

I should have just stayed in bed this morning. My entire life would be different.

Joel's laugh snaps me out of my snit.

"What's so funny?"

"You! I'm not here to tag you."

"You're not?"

"No."

"Oh." I drop my arm. Now he knows I'm an idiot too. Can the day get any worse? "Then why are you here?"

"Well…" It's his turn to blush and look away. Good. I'm not the only loser around this place. "I was wondering if you'd heard about the party."

"Tyson's?"

"Yeah."

"I heard. A Gotcha party. What's next?"

"I know, but the thing is, I need someone to link arms with, and I don't feel like hanging on to one of my guy friends all night, so I was just wondering…" He looks down at my ankle again. "What did you do?"

"It was a snowboarding accident."

"It was?" I can see him trying to puzzle that one out. It was just last night we were at Elijah's house. "But…"

Now it's my turn to laugh at him. "No, loser," I tease. "I tripped. On my schoolbag. Pathetic, huh?"

He laughs. "I once broke my ankle while out walking the dog."

"Really? You tripped too?"

"Sort of. Bailey somehow managed to wrap his leash around my ankles while I was standing there talking to a friend. Then he tore off after a squirrel."

"Oh no!"

"Oh yes." He clamps his ankles together and tilts sideways, reenacting the scene. "I even heard it snap."

"Oh my God."

"Yep. But I considered myself lucky that I didn't break both ankles, or that he didn't drag me all the way down the street. Can you imagine the road rash?"

I laugh, and it feels good. "Okay, you win the pathetic prize."

"Thank you." He grins.

"And my ankle is just sprained. I'm gonna live."

"Glad to hear that. Nice colors, by the way," he adds, referring to the bruising on my ankle.

"Thank you."

The silence that follows is awkward, even though we both pretend to be intent on studying my swollen ankle. I would have painted my toenails last night if I'd known how much attention my feet were going to get today.

"So, about the party. Do you think…?"

And then my mom is in the doorway again, same tray, same mugs of hot chocolate. I decide that it's actually her who wins the pathetic prize, but she scores big points for perseverance.

"Katie, why don't you tell your friend to sit down, stay awhile?" she asks while leaning over and putting the tray on the coffee table. Joel's eyes meet mine and they're smiling, a nice smile.

"Thanks, Mrs. MacLeod," Joel says and sits in the chair. "And thanks for the cookies." He picks one up. "Are these homemade?" he asks, impressed.

"Of course!" my mom says, clearly delighted that he's noticed. "Take as many as you like. I know all about growing boys. I grew up with three brothers."

I roll my eyes, but Joel just smiles again and reaches for another cookie. "These are awesome," he says, devouring the cookie in two bites. "Thank you so much!"

He's either really hungry or he's doing a great job of sucking up. Either way, my mom beams as she watches him reach for a third one. "Please, call me Miriam," she says.

"And I'm Joel. And these are the best cookies I've ever tasted."

"Don't be silly, Joel." Her hand flaps the air once, and I'm surprised to see the blush in her cheeks and the sparkle in her eyes before she lumbers back out of the room.

"So, the party," Joel reminds me. He washes the cookies down with a big gulp of hot chocolate.

"Oh. Right."

I consider my options. Do I really want to go with Joel and face Paige? Will people talk about us, speculating on what our being together means? Do I care?

Joel must think my hesitation is a lack of interest. "It's no big deal," he says, standing up. "It was just a thought."

"No, no!" I tell him. "I'd really like to go. I would. But I had a…a bit of a disagreement with Paige this morning, and if she sees me there with you, she may completely misunderstand."

"What is there to misunderstand?"

"Well…" At first I don't know how much to share with him, but I decide to go with the whole truth. "She wanted me to go with her, you know, linked, but when I pointed out that I'd have to stay seated all evening, she decided that maybe I wouldn't be such a fun person to hang with. So I…I wasn't very nice. I accused her of always wanting to be the center of attention…"

"And that's news?"

"I know! But she didn't like me pointing that out. I really hurt her, and Tanysha and Mariah have taken her side, and, well, the whole thing has been blown totally out of proportion."

Joel thinks about that. "You're going to have to face her sooner or later," he reminds me. "Like at school on Monday."

"I know."

"And at least if you're with me, you won't be facing her alone."

"Facing *them*, you mean."

"Right."

"You sure you don't mind just sitting the whole evening?" I ask. "I'm supposed to keep my foot elevated."

He regards my swollen ankle. "Hmm. Paige may have had a valid point," he says. "That really would be boring. Forget I ever brought it up." He gets up, grabs a cookie for the road and starts toward the door again.

All I can do is gawk. What is with this guy? Then he turns back. He takes one look at my face and bursts out laughing again. "I'd be happy to sit all evening."

"You're bad!"

"No, I'm good. I really had you going for a minute there."

"Bad." I chuck the TV controller at him.

He grabs it out of the air and places it on the table. "So? We'll go together?"

"Maybe."

"Maybe?"

"Yeah, maybe. Like, what happens if you have to go to the bathroom?"

"Same thing as when you have to go to the bathroom."

"Which is?"

"I have to hold it."

"Forget that!"

"Okay then." He smiles. "We temporarily find someone else to link with."

"That could be dangerous."

"It's either that or we go to the bathroom together and one person covers their eyes. We could pretend like we're Siamese twins."

"I think not."

"That would be weird, wouldn't it," Joel muses. "Doing everything together. Not being able to get away from your twin for even one minute. What if you had a fight?"

We regard each other for a moment, considering the situation. "Anyway, forget it," I say, moving on. "I'll take my chances and link with someone else if you go to the bathroom."

"Good plan," he says. "I'll pick you up at eight o'clock."

"You have a car?"

"I'll borrow my mom's." He gets up to leave but then pauses and leans over my ankle. He squeezes the big toe on my injured foot. "And you take it easy."

"I will."

As he heads out of the room I find myself not wanting him to leave. "Joel!" I call.

He turns back. "Yeah?"

I scramble to think of something to say. "Thanks."

"Thanks?"

"Yeah, thanks." But what for? For inviting me to the party? No. "Thanks for not stealing my bead."

He throws his head back and lets out a belly laugh. "Not yet, anyway," he says and winks.

That stumps me. He's gone before I can respond, and I'm left wondering why I hardly ever noticed him between grade one and grade twelve.

I spend the entire afternoon with my trigonometry book open, attempting to tackle this week's assignment, but my mind keeps returning to thoughts of the party. I'll be spending the entire evening linked with Joel. Ahh! What should I wear? I wish I could call Paige. She would know what was appropriate, or, better yet, she would lend me something nice. Yesterday my wardrobe seemed perfectly okay. Today it looks dismal. Eventually I give up on trig and go back to my English Lit novel, *The Handmaid's Tale*.

After dinner I finally decide on my snuggest jeans and the fluttery turquoise blouse that my dad gave me for my last birthday. I look in the mirror and tug at the neckline. Is it too low? Too high? Do I look like some kind of weird butterfly? I use the straightener on my hair and put gold hoops in my ears. I tell myself that I'm just going off to party with the same old gang that I see every day at school, but for the first time in a long time the gang doesn't seem quite as "same old."

The doorbell rings at exactly eight o'clock. Mom hollers up the stairs to tell me Joel is waiting. I squirt my neck with a blast of perfume. Oh no. That was way too much. I scrub my skin with a washcloth. Then I add another coat of lip-gloss. Inspecting myself in the mirror, I see that I'm wearing way too much eye shadow! I take a Q-tip and rub at my eyelids. Then I take the tweezers, and pluck away some more at my eyebrows.

"Katie?" Mom calls again.

"Coming!"

I pull a sock over my good foot but decide to leave the sprained one bare. Any twisting or pressure on it sends lightning bolts of pain up my leg. Did I remember deodorant? I don't think so! Holding my crutches in front of me for balance, I struggle out of my blouse and dab at my armpits with the deodorant stick. Ouch! My armpits are sore from having the crutches grind into them all day. I pull my blouse back on and take a last look in the mirror.

Mom and Joel are both standing at the bottom of the stairs, waiting. Joel is wearing a white shirt, black leather jacket and faded blue jeans. He smiles up at me. Once again I get that surreal feeling that I'm just an actress in a corny movie. Right now I'm supposed to swoon, and I really think I'm going to.

Okay, Katie, get a grip.

I now have to tackle the stairs, and I have to do it with dignity. I try to remember, crutches or foot first? I go to lower my foot first. No, it's crutches first, obviously. I manage the first step. Then the second. The stairs are looking particularly steep this evening. I managed them earlier, but no one was watching me then, especially not Joel. I take the third step, but I suddenly have a vision of what would happen if I swung my weight down the wrong way on the crutches. I'd go head over heels, crashing all the way to the bottom. Then I'd have a fractured neck, and not just a sprained ankle.

I feel my cheeks burn. I have no idea how to proceed. Who is this nervous stranger that has invaded my body?

"You can do it, Katie," Joel encourages.

His gentle voice relaxes me, and I become aware of how ridiculously I'm behaving. Who am I trying to impress? "Forget this," I tell them. I send one crutch sliding down the stairs, and then the other. Extending my injured ankle out in front of me, I sit on the third step and bounce my bum the rest of the way down.

"Katie, you'll wear a hole in your jeans," my mom scolds.

Joel just laughs and passes my crutches back to me. "I like your style," he says.

He holds the front door open while I clomp outside. I try to ignore Mom's goofy grin. For a woman who has always warned me about making hasty first impressions, she's decided Joel is a good guy awfully damn fast, and all because he liked her cookies.

"Have fun you two," she calls as we're getting into the car.

"We will, Miriam," Joel assures her. "And we won't be too late." He waves as we pull out of the driveway. Mom waves back.

"You just want more of her cookies, Mr. Suck-up,"
I tease.

"Damn right," he agrees, and we both laugh. I can feel
myself descending back to that easy place we were at this
afternoon. I sink into the seat and breathe deeply. Joel hums
to the tune on the radio and lightly taps the steering wheel.
Why had I gotten into such a tizzy over this? I find myself
rubbing the bead that's on the chain around my neck.

"Still got yours?" I ask.

He glances over to see what I'm talking about. "Of course."

"You never know."

"You're right. Forty people have lost theirs."

"Really?" That's a lot more than Paige told me about.
"How do you know?"

"Warren has set up a group page on Facebook with all
our names on it."

"Are you serious?"

"Yeah. It's great. If you get tagged you leave the group.
Then the rest of us know who is still in."

"Who else has lost their beads?"

"Did you hear about Michelle?"

"Yep."

"Kerry?"

"Uh-huh."

"How about Taia?"

"No. Who got her?"

"Anthony. Marc told her that he knew for sure that
Caitlin had her name, so when Anthony phoned her and

asked if he could come over and borrow her English notes, she thought it was safe. Turns out Anthony actually paid Marc ten dollars to tell her that."

"Are you serious?"

"Yep."

"I've only heard about girls who've lost their beads. Are there any boys?"

"Yeah, a few. You'll have to check for yourself."

"So, with this group page, what keeps people from saying they're out when they're really still in?"

"Why would they do that?"

"So that their victims would let their guard down when they're around."

"Hmm." He thinks about that. "I guess people could do that, but someone else would post a rebuttal. There's a lot of people posting notes on the wall."

"But you wouldn't know which one of them was lying."

Joel glances over at me. "You're not a very trusting person, are you, Katie?"

"Not when it comes to Gotcha," I tell him.

He nods. "Yeah, I guess the proof is in the beads. You can either show them or you can't."

We drive along in comfortable silence for a minute or two. Then Joel asks, "So, do you have any strategies you're willing to share?"

"And why would I share them with you?"

"Because when we were in grade two I always let you butt in front of me in line."

"You did not!"

"I did too! You don't remember?"

"No!" I laugh at the thought of it and then study his face to see if he's serious. I can't tell. His lips are turned up at the corners, but that's their normal state. "What line?"

"The one at lunchtime. I was usually waiting for a soccer ball. I think you always took a skipping rope."

"Probably," I agree. I was useless at sports.

"I'm devastated," he says. "I was being my most gentlemanly self, and you didn't even notice."

"So why did you let me butt in?" I ask. I'm sure he's teasing me again, but I decide to play along.

"Because you were the cutest girl in second grade."

"Oh shut up!"

"You were! Your pigtails really were pigs' tails. They were these two perfect coils on either side of your head. I always had to resist the urge to pull on them, just to see them spring back up."

It's true, my mom did always tie my hair up that way. How did he remember that?

"And you had the sweetest smile. I remember how hard I had to work to make you laugh, though. You were so shy."

"Seven-year-old boys don't notice the girls."

"I did."

"Hmm."

He looks me over. "You've grown, Katie."

I laugh. "You too, Joel. Just a bit."

"So you owe me. What's your strategy?"

I still don't know if he was making that all up, but I decide to humor him. "My strategy is not to get in the game until it pays big."

"Huh?"

"I'll wait until my victim has amassed enough beads that it's worth the trouble."

"Interesting strategy," Joel says. "And how is your victim doing?"

"I'm not sure," I tell him honestly. "If I don't find out tonight, I guess I'll have to check Facebook later."

"And assume everyone is telling the truth."

"Right."

"Not a bad strategy. But not much fun, either."

"What's your strategy?"

"I don't really have one. I'm just trying to stay in the game as long as possible, but I don't expect to win."

"Why not?"

"Because I'm not hungry enough for the money. All we each lose is ten dollars, but with some people you'd think their life savings was tied up in the game."

"Maybe that is the life savings of some people."

"Could be." He smiles. "But I find it interesting to watch how crazy people get when they're playing a game. It's all or nothing. I can't really relate."

Neither can I. I decide to ask Joel his opinion on something that has been bothering me. "Do you think Warren and Paige and I could get suspended for running the game? Fetterly made it clear it wasn't to be a grad activity this year."

Joel shakes his head. "No, they'd have to suspend everyone who was playing it, all two hundred and twelve of us."

I hope he's right. At some point it dawned on me that a suspension noted on my permanent school record wouldn't impress too many colleges.

When we pull up outside Tyson's house, Joel leaps out of the car and grabs my crutches from the backseat. He hands them to me, and when I'm balanced, he wraps an arm securely around one crutch. "I guess this is how we're going to have to link," he says.

"Yeah," I say, for lack of any better ideas.

"But I think I'm going to have to place my hand over yours on the crutch grip," he says. "I don't know what else to do with it. Is that okay?"

Before I can answer, his hand is warm on mine, and that swooning feeling is back. You'd think I was thirteen years old.

We make our way awkwardly up the path to the front door. I think of mentioning that we don't need to be linked yet because there is no one else outside, but I'm enjoying the warmth of his hand on mine, and it's fun trying to get into the rhythm of walking linked, with a set of crutches to maneuver.

The linked team of Tyson and Jason open the door, and if they're surprised to see us together, neither one says so. As we make our way into the kitchen, I feel myself tensing up again, expecting to see Paige. I look around the crowded room, but it seems she hasn't arrived yet. The music is loud and I can see lots of people dancing in the living room, many of them with their arms strung through someone else's. It makes for some pretty goofy dance moves.

"I'd get us a couple of drinks," Joel yells into my ear, "but I don't know how I can carry them and move around linked to you."

"Then we'll have to stand beside the bar to drink and sit when we're not."

"Do you want something now?"

I look around to see what's available. There are beer and soda cans, liquor bottles and sticky-looking shot glasses scattered across the counter. When we arrived, Tyson told us that his older brother had done a run to the liquor store for us earlier and there was a cooler full of beverages that we could buy off him. Tyson's girlfriend, who's not in grade twelve, is sitting on a stool beside the cooler, collecting money. His parents both work in the travel industry and are away a lot, so he and his brother have become party-throwing experts. I consider asking for a cooler, thinking it might relax me, but decide that I don't need anything that might make me even wobblier than I already am on crutches. I took a strong painkiller before we left, and I'm having enough trouble balancing as it is. "Not right now," I yell back at him. I can feel my ankle throbbing and really want to put it up somewhere. "But if you want something, go ahead."

"I don't want anything either. It would just make me have to pee, and you know how that would complicate things." He grins down at me. "Let's go over to the kitchen table and insist that a couple of able-bodied people give up their chairs for us," he shouts in my ear. "There's got to be some advantage in hanging with you tonight."

I retaliate by elbowing him in the ribs, and then we gracelessly cross the room together. Amy and Megan rise as a linked pair and give us their chairs. Someone else pushes an ottoman into the kitchen for me to rest my foot on. Joel slides his chair close to mine so we can comfortably stay linked.

As people come through the kitchen, everyone asks about my ankle. Over and over I describe my fabricated snowboarding accident. It's harmless and way more entertaining and less klutzy sounding than tripping on a schoolbag. Joel enhances my story, even claiming to be right there when it happened.

"You should have seen her," he says. "She went off a jump, did a twist in the air, looked set for a perfect landing and then wham!" He slams his palm on the table and gives a vivid description of my wipeout, and even I am impressed by what a spectacular one it was. No one seems to remember that I'm not the athletic type and that snowboarding would be right out of the question. There is just complete admiration that I could take such a spill and live to tell the tale. With each retelling, we embellish the story a little.

"It was a double black run," Joel says.

"And as I was rolling over and over, heading toward the cliff face," I add, "all I could think about was my bead and how it might rip off and get lost in the snow."

The party gets louder as more drinks are consumed. I don't see any beads being captured, but then people are not leaving themselves exposed. Those who have already lost their beads are the only ones free to move from room to room alone. Linked couples flow in and out of the kitchen, and each pair stops by the table to inquire about my elevated foot. By the eighth rendition, I find myself marveling at how easily Joel and I are able to play off one another. We're a great team. I'm so absorbed in our little fantasy that I'm unaware of the arrival of some new partiers who are now standing behind us, listening. Someone decides to change the CD, and as the party noise diminishes momentarily, a familiar voice cuts through the room.

"A snowboarding accident?"

Everyone turns to see who is speaking.

Paige is linked with Tanysha but still manages to strike an authoritative pose. "And here I thought you simply tripped over your schoolbag."

Six

That's all it takes, one snarky comment from Paige and the laid-back, cheerful party atmosphere completely changes. It's like she's the mood dictator. If she's in the mood to party, we can have fun. If she's ticked off, so is everyone else. The room gets completely still, and I can feel the tension build as people look from her to me. I'm tempted to turn to her and say, *"See? There you go again, stealing all the attention!"* but somehow I resist.

Joel and I make eye contact, and I wonder if we can telepathically plan our next move. I see the spark in his eyes, and then his palm slaps the table again. He throws his head back and laughs, hard. "I can't believe we had so many of you guys going!" he says, looking around. Then he turns to Paige. "And you! You ruined our little game. And here I always thought you were a good sport."

I decide to follow suit. "I don't even snowboard," I tell the room. "Not ever, not even once." I laugh too, hoping it doesn't sound half as phony as it is. No one laughs with me, and the room gets quieter still. The atmosphere feels menacing. What's with these guys? It was just a joke. I would have told the truth eventually. Maybe. And anyway, who really cares?

Tyson is leaning against a kitchen counter, still linked with Jason. "Very funny, you two," he says. "You had me fooled."

"Thanks," Joel says, bowing his head.

"What I'm wondering now," Tyson says, "is how bad Katie's ankle really is. Maybe we should make her get up, alone, and walk across the kitchen, just to prove it's sprained."

He sounds like Captain Hook, ordering me to walk the plank.

There's a chorus of "yeahs!" around the room. I'm surprised. Being elected to grad council immediately elevates your social status, and there's a level of protection that goes with that. People don't mess with me.

"Hey," Joel says. He leans forward and tugs on the hem of my jeans, exposing more of my swollen ankle. "Just look at it. She could really mess it up if she did that."

"Maybe," Tyson says. "And she might lose her bead, too, which would be fair punishment for sucking us all in, don't you think?" he asks, looking around the room for support.

There's raucous applause, whistles and more "yeahs!"

Someone turns off the music. All eyes are fixed on the little kangaroo court playing itself out in the kitchen.

"C'mon, Tyson," Joel argues. "It was just a joke."

That prompts Tyson to turn his attention to Joel. "And for being Katie's sidekick," he suggests, "I think Joel has to remain unlinked and alone during Katie's trek around the kitchen."

The cheers and wolf whistles escalate. I'm reminded of a lynching. How did the party atmosphere turn this mean-spirited so quickly? I know Paige's presence has a strong influence, but something else has taken over here. My classmates have become vulture-like, circling their prey. I force myself to appear relaxed because I know instinctively that, just like animals, if they smell my fear, they'll grow even more malicious. It's not so much losing my bead that I'm worried about, but the pack mentality that has possessed them.

Joel must sense it too. Gotcha has a reputation for turning vicious. "Very funny, Tyson," he says, rising from his chair and pulling me up with him. "But if you can't take a joke, I feel sorry for you. We were just having a little fun that has nothing to do with Gotcha, so I don't feel one bit obliged to follow through on your stupid punishment. It's been a great party, but I think it's time for us to move on, so if you'll excuse us…"

With Joel latched onto my arm, I turn toward the hallway that leads to the front entrance but come face to face with Paige and company, who are blocking the door. Despite Paige's small stature, they're standing firm. I hesitate, wondering if we should just push past them, and in that split second I feel the circle of grads growing tighter around us. Tyson and Jason lurch over, and Tyson begins tugging on the crutch that Joel's not linked to. Joel reaches around me with his free hand and shoves Tyson, but with only one leg to stand on for balance, I quickly lose the tug-o-war.

Tyson passes my crutch to someone standing behind him and then grabs the one that Joel and I are sharing. I struggle to keep my balance, knowing how painful it will be to put weight on my foot, but I finally give up my grip. Joel doesn't. He continues to fight Tyson for the crutch, with me clinging to his arm. The room explodes with cheering.

"Just give it to him!" I yell into Joel's ear.

He either doesn't hear or chooses to ignore me. I throw my arms around his waist, fighting to remain upright. People behind Tyson pull on him, creating an advantage, and now Joel falls forward, taking me with him. He lets go of the crutch and we crash to the floor. I scream as my ankle twists under me. The room erupts with applause and cheering. Joel and I untangle ourselves, and he quickly tucks his arm through mine while I hunch over, cradling my throbbing foot in both hands. It's only fear that's keeping me from sobbing in agony. I look up at a sea of monster faces laughing down at me, like in a nightmare. Tyson's swinging the crutch over his head and dragging Jason around the kitchen in a dance of victory. Then I feel hands all over me, trying to pry me away from Joel. We cling to each other, anger fueling my strength, but I can feel myself losing my grip. I look at Joel and see panic on his face. His hands clutch at my arms, but there are too many people pulling on him, pulling on me...

And then a familiar voice booms out over the ruckus. "What the hell is going on in here?"

There's a hush and Joel and I are released. We all turn to stare at the imposing figure who has replaced Paige and gang in the doorway. It's Warren, class president, and he's linked with Jenna.

"Well?" he asks in a voice that commands an answer.

But no one says a word. It's like Warren's voice has dropped us back into the real world, where people are civilized. Paige may be the mood czar, but Warren's voice works like a slap of cold water, startling us out of this crazy hallucination. I look around at the faces of my classmates. Expressions that were hostile and vicious just one minute ago have become sheepish, and no one makes eye contact with anyone else. The rush of adrenaline that precipitated the mobbing is retreating as quickly as it arrived, and I sense no one really understands what just happened.

Joel climbs to his feet and bends over to help me up. The pain shooting from my ankle is intense, and I'm afraid I'll keel over if I get up too quickly.

"Katie, you okay?" Warren asks, spotting me on the floor.

I can only shake my head, and I stay where I am. Joel sinks back down beside me, linking my arm protectively. Someone passes my crutches to him, and the volume on the stereo is turned back up. I can hear the *psst* from beer cans as they are cracked open, and the party slowly resumes. Everyone moves away from where I'm still sprawled out, as dignified as a squashed spider.

Warren comes over and squats in front of me, pulling Jenna down with him. "What happened, Katie?" he asks, looking concerned. His buttery smooth voice almost makes me forget my pain. Almost.

"Just an attempted assassination," I tell him.

"Huh?"

I shake my head. "I pissed Tyson off, and he was trying to get even." I look around and the party is back on track, as if nothing had happened. "I can't believe these people."

"Was it about your bead?"

"Sort of."

"You still have it?"

"Yeah."

He gently runs a finger across my ankle, which I've stretched out in front of me. "Whew!" he exclaims and whistles softly. "Did this just happen now?"

Oh man. Just as Warren begins to get to me with his intoxicating voice, charm and knight-in-shining-armor-to-the-rescue style, I remember why I've never been attracted to him. He's not very bright. It's too bad.

"No, Warren," I explain, as patiently as I can given the pain I'm in. "It takes a while for an ankle to get that swollen and bruised."

He nods.

"I came on those crutches."

"Oh yeah. Right."

"Thanks for coming along when you did," I add, feeling a twinge of guilt for what I know is soon to be a traitorous act.

"You're welcome." He grins like a little boy, pleased with himself. Now I feel even worse about what I know I have to do, sooner or later.

As he stands back up, I wonder if he has a better under-standing of how he stopped the mini-riot than those who were part of it understand how it happened. Does he purposely command respect or does it just happen when he opens his mouth? Either way, I'm glad he did.

Joel and I slowly climb back up, and with my crutches firmly under my arms, we slink out of the house and back to his car.

"Katie," he says, turning to me before starting the engine. "I'm so sorry."

"Hey, not your fault." And it wasn't. But I'm feeling so mortified and abused and foolish that I can't look at him. I just want to be home, in my bed, with my head buried under my pillow. I clench my teeth, willing the flood of tears I know is coming to hold off a little longer.

"I brought you to the party and I helped create the story. I feel responsible."

I rub my face with my hands and press my fingers into my eyes, a dam to the tears. My ankle's throbbing. My head's aching. I take a deep breath. "Joel, it's the game. You said your-self that people get crazy playing Gotcha. I'm dropping out."

Joel starts the car and pulls away from the curb. "Do you think they'll let you?"

"How can they stop me?"

"I don't know. But who would get your bead and the name of your victim?"

"Whoever I give them to. You."

"Somehow I don't think we'd get away with that, espe-cially after the episode tonight."

I can only shrug. Right now I don't care. I need pain-killers so badly, and I want to get my foot elevated. How could an evening that started off so special turn sour this fast? I don't even want to think about Gotcha anymore.

Joel helps me unlock the door to my house. "You're going to be okay?" he asks, handing me my key.

I nod, but I still can't look at him. It's getting harder to hold back the tears, but I don't want Joel to know how I'm feeling. It will just make him feel worse.

He hesitates, blocking the doorway, and I get the feeling he wants to say something else. But there's nothing else to say. The awkwardness is too much.

"Joel, I need to go in. My foot is killing me."

He jumps out of the way. "Sorry, Katie," he says, sounding almost defensive. He moves out of the way and holds the door for me.

"Bye, Joel," I say and pull the door shut behind me. I slump against the wall and unleash the tears.

Mom has gone to bed but she's left some lights on and a plate of cookies on the counter. She must have figured I'd invite Joel in. When the sobbing finally lets up, I drag myself off the floor and swallow a couple of Tylenol. I'm exhausted, totally spent, my eyes are burning, my ankle's throbbing, but I know I won't sleep until the painkillers kick in. I decide to check my e-mail while I'm waiting.

From: dannyo56@hotmail.com
To: kittiekat17@hotmail.com
Subject: sprained ankle

Hey Katie,

How is your ankle doing? It breaks my heart to hear you
sounding so down.

Listen, honey, I know you're feeling the pinch, money-
wise, but do you have any cash at all? The reason I'm
asking is I've just been given a hot tip on an investment that
promises to triple your money almost overnight. I have very
little to invest myself, but I'm sharing this tip with everyone
I know. Depending on what you have, it just might be your
ticket to the finest of grad dresses, maybe even college
tuition.

Anyway, I hope you're feeling better, and let me know
about this opportunity. Keep that pretty chin up!

Love Dad

PS. Your father has not left you, your mother is not a cow,
and you have a great future ahead of you.

From: kittiekat17@hotmail.com
To: dannyo56@hotmail.com
Subject: Re: sprained ankle

drop dead

Serious agony finally drags me out of bed and into the bathroom, where my next dose of painkillers await me. Given the kind of day it's been, I would have expected it to be one of those nights where I tossed and turned relentlessly, torturing myself with regrets and thinking of the perfect comebacks for things that were said. But no. Tonight any body movement at all—even from my upper body—disturbs the quilt, which then slides across my foot, and even that light caress causes me to jolt awake with the pain. I'm forced to lie flat on my back without twitching a muscle. It doesn't make for a restful sleep. I've been staring at the ceiling for hours.

But now it's safe to take a couple more Tylenol. I'd thought of leaving them on my night table so I wouldn't have to get up, but it's impossible to carry a glass of water, or anything, when you're using crutches. I left them on the bathroom counter, and I swallow them by bending over the sink and drinking water directly from the flowing tap. I'd like to get a fresh ice pack, but it's too far to go to the kitchen.

Sitting on the side of my bed with my reading light glowing, I take a closer look at my ankle. It looks much the same as it did late yesterday afternoon, even though it is hurting so much more. The banging around at the party probably aggravated the damage that was already done.

I gently place the quilt over my foot and lie back, waiting for the pills to begin their magic. I'm going to ask Mom if she can get me something stronger tomorrow. These pills help, but not enough.

As I begin to float back into a semiconscious state, I think of Dad's e-mail. It's been ten days since I've seen him. I try to picture his face in my mind, with his kind smile and warm brown eyes. My response to his note will bring sadness to those eyes. I feel a twinge of guilt.

When I was younger, Dad never worked at one job for very long, so we hung out a lot. He loves the outdoors and we'd go on what he called explorations. Our town is nestled in a valley, so when the weather was good we'd pack a picnic and go hiking. I loved the feeling of my small hand in his large one as we walked along the wooded trails. He often pulled me into a squat and we'd carefully examine wildflowers or mushroom clusters, noticing how exquisite each one of Mother Nature's gifts was. We'd rest often, admiring the meandering mountain streams or the way the early morning sunlight filtered through the trees and mist, slashing the air with gray stripes.

When we sat down on a fallen log or rocky outcrop to eat our peanut butter and honey sandwiches, we'd play "name that bird." I glowed right down to my toes when Dad gave me that look that said I'd correctly identified a bird by its song. Occasionally one would stump us, and Dad would pull the bird book from the backpack and we'd pore through it, looking for possibilities. Out of the pack would also come the binoculars, and we'd peer into the foliage, looking for a bird whose plumage matched the pictures in the book.

On sticky summer days, Dad would plunk me in a child carrier on the back of his bike and we'd cycle on the bike paths around town, letting the breeze dry our skin. I'd lay my cheek on his strong back and doze, and then we'd stop for ice-cream cones, chocolate fudge for me, French vanilla for him. Sometimes we took Paige on our outings. Her dad and mine were friends, and Dad wanted me to have company my own age.

Feeling stiff, I try to plump up my pillow without moving my legs too much. I end up just flipping it over and then press my cheek into the cool pillowcase, sinking back into Dad thoughts. When did this idyllic childhood begin to unravel?

It wasn't until I was in school, a few years later, that I grew aware of how miserable Mom became when Dad wasn't working, so when I'd come home and find him lying on the couch, unshaven, newspapers scattered around the living room, I'd do a quick pick-up-and-tidy routine so she wouldn't go ballistic. Those were the days he started going out after dinner instead of hanging with me, and he wouldn't be home until after I was in bed. I didn't ask where he went. There was something about Mom's body language that gave me the feeling it was a taboo subject.

Before he left, Dad had started spending every morning at the computer. He called himself a day trader. I didn't really understand what he was doing, but it was nice to see him so interested in something again, and it made him happy. But Mom didn't like seeing him happy. She accused him of throwing away our money. He kept bizarre hours, waking early to "work" at the computer, sleeping all afternoon and then going out again after dinner to who knows where. When he did get home, late, I could hear them through the bedroom wall. She was all over him, blaming, accusing, threatening...

I guess I shouldn't have been so surprised when he finally packed up and left. I just wish he'd taken me with him.

Seven

'm staying in bed, maybe forever. Mom's hauling herself up and down the stairs, bringing me food and painkillers. She asked about the party on her first visit, but my curt response shut her up. I also told her I wasn't taking phone calls or going back to school. She looked concerned but kept her thoughts to herself and simply tucked my ratty old stuffed bunny under the quilt with me.

I've watched the light in the room change as the day has dragged on, and I can tell without even looking at the clock that it's late afternoon. One day closer to the end of the school year and my freedom from all things crazy, like Gotcha. And grad. Do I even want to attend graduation ceremonies with people who can turn into savages at the slightest provocation? I don't think so. They may blame it on the game, but the panic I felt last night when they'd worked themselves into that frenzy and were swarming Joel and me…well, they're all lunatics.

Except Joel. Joel Keister. I feel smiley just thinking of him. I pull the stuffed bunny out from under my quilt and caress his satin ears. Joel's the only sane one. I remember the warmth of his arm pressing against mine last night. For a while we were totally connected, playing our own private game. The empty ache I've had since Dad left evaporated as we leaned into each other, allowing that warm current to run between us. When he looked at me it was as though he was really seeing me, and I was seeing him.

I feel a stab of remorse as I remember how our evening ended, and I chuck the bunny across the room. It hits the wall, drops onto its head and sprawls helplessly on the floor, looking just as stupid as I did last night. That was the most humiliating moment of my life. And so then what did I do? I pushed Joel away when he was being kind and caring. I bet he hates me. I should call him, tell him it's me who's sorry. I started the stupid story. He got it, and he totally understood why I had to make something up. And then when all hell broke loose, he stuck with me. That's more than I can say for Paige. I bet she was gloating when she saw what they were going to do to us. It's like she cast an evil spell on the whole room.

The most recent dose of painkillers is finally working. I can roll over onto my side without causing spasms of pain to run up my leg. I punch my pillow, trying to fluff it back up, and I pull the quilt over my shoulders.

What's happening to us? We were just a normal class of kids, getting ready to move into the next phase of our lives. It's creepy how Gotcha has changed us, or some of us. Is it because we expected it to, or is it the way the game is played that creates the bizarre behavior? If it had been someone else who was being ganged up on last night would I have participated? God, I hope not.

My back finally starts aching from lying in bed for so long and I have to get up. Somewhere between my bed and my bum-hop down the stairs, I decide that now is the time to follow through on the decision I made last night. I clomp my way over to the phone in the kitchen. I can hear the drone of the TV in the living room, meaning Mom's not going to over-hear my phone call. Good. I'll be spared the "I told you so's."

I quickly dial the number. Warren answers after the first ring, and the resonance of his voice jump-starts that familiar stir deep in my stomach. What is wrong with me? I'll blame it on the painkillers.

"Warren, it's me, Katie."

"Hey, Kittiekat."

I hate it when people use my dad's nickname for me, but hearing Warren say it now…well, it gives it a certain…style.

"How's your ankle?" he asks.

"Not very good. It hurts."

"That's too bad. How did you say you did it?"

"Just a stupid accident." I'm surprised no one told him the story of what happened before he arrived at the party, but then again, as we were leaving, everyone was acting like nothing had happened.

"So, you were at Tyson's with Joel Keister?"

"Yeah. Paige is mad at me, and Joel needed someone to link with." I don't know why I feel the need to explain it to him, but I do.

"Oh."

Oh? What does he mean by that? Time to get to the point of my call. "Warren, I'm…I'm dropping out of the game."

There's a long pause. "Out of Gotcha?"

"Right."

Another long pause. "You can't do that, Kittiekat. Once you're in, the only way out is to lose your bead."

"Oh yeah? Who says?"

"No one drops out of Gotcha. It's the rules."

"Show me where they're written."

I can hear him sigh. "The rules aren't written anywhere, you know that. But they've been passed down over the years."

"Well that's stupid! I don't want my money back or anything. I just want out."

"That's not going to happen."

"I'll give my bead away, and my name. It's no big deal."

"But someone has your name, Katie."

And I have someone's name, I think to myself but don't mention. "Then I'll give that person my bead."

"And deprive them of their fun, as well as giving them a freebie? That won't go over very well with the rest of the class, and I think you know what happens when you anger the Gotcha Gods."

The Gotcha Gods? "Oh c'mon, Warren. It's just a stupid game." But suddenly I'm thinking he knows more about last night than he's letting on. And maybe he knew exactly what he was doing when he defused the situation with just his voice. Is there more to Warren than I thought?

"No, you c'mon, Katie," he says and then adds, more gently, "Just hang in there a little longer. You'll be tagged soon enough."

"No! I'm not playing."

Warren doesn't answer, so I continue. "Okay then. I'll let it be known that I'm...I'm going to stand on the street, near the school, and whoever has my name can just come and get my bead."

"I can't stop you from doing that."

"Good."

There's another long pause. His lack of response is making me nervous. It causes me to babble on. "I actually think we should stop the whole game now before someone gets hurt."

Warren laughs. It's a beautiful laugh, yet it makes me feel queasy. "Not a chance, Kittiekat."

"My name's Katie. And just for the record, Warren, if something goes wrong, real wrong, it's on your shoulders. I'm not part of it anymore."

"That's where you're mistaken, Katie." He says my name with emphasis. "We're all in this together."

"Not for much longer."

"Whatever you say, Katie."

I slam down the phone. Jerk! He saw what was happening last night. He knows it's only going to get worse as we get closer to the end. I lied when I said it was "just a game."

It's not. Not at all. I could never understand how things got so bad in other years, but now I'm starting to get it.

It's Wednesday and I still have my bead, but only because I haven't been to school. Even if I wanted to go, I have no way of getting there as Mom leaves too early in the morning to drive me, and I can't walk that far with crutches. I'm overdosing on talk-show TV, with all the freaks and idiots, and it's scaring me. I could be one of those loser guests in a few years.

"And you say it all started when you sprained your ankle?"

"Yes. That's when it started."

"And after that you had no friends and you started flunking out in school?"

"Yes. That's exactly what happened."

"You claim you were a popular, straight-A student before you tripped on your schoolbag."

"I'm not 'claiming' I was! I totally was!"

"And you say you were ganged up on in a grad activity, in a game called Gotcha."

"Yes, that's what happened. And it was awful! They wanted me to walk on my sprained ankle…"

"Hmm. It seems strange that a sprained ankle could keep you from graduating and going on to college…"

"Well it did! And it was because of the beads! And those people who came to my door. And then everyone went crazy…"

"Well, Katie, we have a surprise guest here today. She was your best friend before you sprained your ankle, and we're now going to hear her side of the story. She says that your flunking out had nothing to do with your sprained ankle, but was because you were spreading untrue rumors about her."

The TV audience shrieks its approval. I cover my ears...

I find myself checking my e-mail constantly, hoping to hear from Dad. Finally I give in and write to him.

From: kittiekat17@hotmail.com
To: dannyo56@hotmail.com
Subject: Re: sprained ankle

hi dad,

im sorry bout my last email. i was havin a really bad night. the gotcha game is gettin crazy. ppl r goin insane. my ankle is really sore so i cant get 2 school which is bad b/c i need 2 keep my marks up 2 get those scholarships + i cant work so im not making N E $ 2 put towards school tuition or even a grad dress. i guess thats my excuse 4 being so angry. im also havin friendship problems. i feel like ive been pushed in2 1 of those waterslide chutes, i'm sliding down, away from everything good & theres no turning back til i drop out the bottom. w/ my luck, there will only b a pile of jagged rocks there & no pool of water.

or there will b a talk-show host wanting 2 make a fool of me.

i hope things r going better for u.
katie

From: dannyo56@hotmail.com
To: kittiekat17@hotmail.com
Subject: Re: sprained ankle

Dear Katie,

I'm sorry you're having a tough time. But remember, it's up to you to decide to be happy. No one else can do that for you. Enjoy that slide! Envision a fragrant bubble bath at the bottom, and it will be yours. (And what's this about a talk-show host?)

About the money woes, have you given any more thought to me investing your money for you? I'm still confident that I can make you some cash, fast.

Take care, sweetheart.
Dad

It's Thursday and I'm at the kitchen table, staring out the window. The snowcapped mountain peaks in the distance shimmer in the morning sun, and the daffodil shoots in the window box are on the verge of bursting into bloom. The sun has warmed the room until it's toasty. In my past life, the one where I had a future and friends and an intact family, a dew-sparkling morning like this always energized me and made me feel like anything could happen. But today the morning feels as drab as any other. The angle of the sun shows how grimy the windows are. I can't make myself a decent break-fast because, with my crutches, I can't carry anything from the fridge to the counter, and if I make toast or warm something in the microwave, I have to stand at the counter to eat it. I'm now missing my fourth day of school, and it's going to be hell to catch up. I've read every book in the house, no one has brought me any assignments or notes from school, and I can only look forward to twelve more hours of daytime soaps or talk shows.

And Joel hasn't called.

I switch on the computer and read the online horoscope that pops up on our home page. *Step out of your comfort zone and take a chance today. You never know until you try.* Oh yeah, that's helpful. I can't *step* anywhere.

I reread my dad's last e-mail. I wonder about this money-making tip he's talking about. Mom used to accuse him of losing all their money. Would he take any chances with mine? I don't think so. He knows how much I need it. I do have about $900 in my savings account, mostly from the tips I've earned at the restaurant and which I busted my butt for. But this is nothing compared to what I'll need for tuition and books and living-out expenses. I decide to check my bank account online to see exactly how much there is.

I log into the secure area of the bank web page and type in my password. A screen appears with my personal information. Whoa! Something's wrong. The computer shows that there's $3,105.38 in my account. That's not right. I close the screen and log on again. It still shows $3,105.38. Where did it come from? An anonymous donor?

And then I remember. I put the Gotcha money in my account. For a second there I thought I really did have a fairy godmother. I'm so pathetic. I should withdraw it and turn it over to someone else to keep. I don't want any part of that game. It's blood money.

An idea comes to me, slowly worming its way into my consciousness while I stare at the computer screen. What if I lend Dad the Gotcha money? He could invest it and then... what was it he said? It would triple overnight? I do the math in my head. I'd give the Gotcha winner their $2,120 and keep the rest. That would be over $4,000! My heart pitter-patters at the thought of it. No one would have to know. I'd be able to buy the most beautiful dress for grad—if I decide to go. And that's a big if. But at least I wouldn't have to wear something secondhand, and there'd still be lots left over.

Do I dare? I feel a shiver of excitement. That would be such poetic justice. A way to get even with all those crazy people from the party.

Step out of your comfort zone and take a chance today. You never know until you try.

I smile. I have the astrologer's blessing. And Dad says you have to choose to be happy. I thought he was being corny, but now I've decided he's right. And not only can I choose to be happy, I can choose to make some easy money. The thought of it energizes me and I laugh out loud. There, I'm already way happier, and I haven't even done anything yet.

I e-mail my dad.

He shows up an hour later.

"Hey, Kittiekat," he says after letting himself in the front door with his key. He leans over and kisses my forehead.

I'm stunned. I haven't seen the guy for nearly two weeks, and suddenly he's here. And he looks like hell. He's unshaven, his eyes are red-rimmed, and his clothes look like he's been sleeping in them for the past two weeks. For the first time ever, I see him as a man, almost a stranger, and not my sweet and gentle daddy who once gave me piggyback rides to bed and then stayed with me, stroking my hair, until I grew drowsy.

"How's your ankle?" he asks, touching it lightly. I'm on the couch and my foot is elevated and bare. The bruising has become increasingly colorful as the week has progressed.

"It's not as bad as it was, though it's looking worse all the time," I tell him as calmly as I can, yet it's taking a huge effort to swallow the hurt I'm feeling and act normal, like it's not weird that he's suddenly here. Does he think I won't notice that he never bothered to drop by until I found some money for him to invest, and then he's here almost immediately? I've missed him desperately, ached for him, but this is not the way I thought our reunion would happen. I wanted him to come and see me just because he wants to, because he misses me, not for any other reason.

"I've missed you so much, Katie," he says. He's studying me, probably reading my thoughts. I have to look away. "And I wanted to come and see you," he says. "But it was so hard to leave, and I was afraid that if I came back I wouldn't be able to go again."

I have nothing to say to that.

"So, where did you get this money from, the money you want to invest?" he asks, wisely changing the subject.

"It's the prize money for the Gotcha game. All the grads who are playing put in ten dollars, and the winner takes all."

"Sounds like fun."

"It's not."

"No?"

"It's crazy. People will actually hurt other people to get their bead."

"That's not good."

"No, it's not."

"Maybe there should be some more rules instigated, like no hurting each other." He laughs at the absurdity of his own comment.

"So where are you living, Dad?"

"I don't want to talk about that, Kittiekat."

"Why not?"

He looks at me sadly. "Just because," he says.

I had convinced myself that he was living with another woman, and that's why he wouldn't let me come for a visit, but now that I can see the shape he's in, I know that's not the case. He looks more like he's been living on the streets.

"How's your mom?" he asks sadly.

"The same."

"She's a good lady," he tells me. "I miss her too."

"Then why don't you come home?"

"Not yet, Kittiekat. I have to prove to both of you that I can make something more of myself."

"You don't have to prove anything to me, Dad."

"Thanks, Katie. But I have to prove something to myself."

He does? I wonder what that would be. Maybe that he can be happy as a homeless person?

"So?" he asks. "I take it the money is in your bank account?"

"Yep."

"And you still want to invest it?"

"Uh-huh." Though now that I can see the shape he's in, I'm having my doubts. This man does not look like my dad. He's acting strange, coming over only when I have some money for him. Can I still trust him?

"Then I guess we need to get over to the bank."

I try stalling. "Do you want to stay for a bit, have a shower, get a change of clothes…?"

Dad looks around. "I'd love to, Katie. I would. But that will just make it much harder to leave again."

I sigh. I know I can't change my mind now, not to his face. "Okay then. Pass me my crutches."

Thirty minutes later I'm back on the couch, alone again. We've been to the bank. I've withdrawn the money and given it to Dad. The adrenaline rush I had when I decided to give him the Gotcha money is gone, and I feel miserable. I know it wasn't my money to give away, and Dad was acting so strange. What have I done now?

Yet Dad assured me I'd have it back in a week, two at the outside. That's a little longer than the "overnight" that he promised me initially, but it won't matter because Gotcha will run at least that much longer. I know Dad won't let me down in this. He won't.

I can't believe how quickly he left. He engulfed me in a hug at the door when he brought me back from the bank, and I swear I saw tears in his eyes when he said good-bye, but he clearly wanted to get away from our house as fast as he could. It would have been nice if he'd made me some lunch, and we could have talked, catching up on the past two weeks. He knows Mom's gone all day. He doesn't have a job to go to, or a home, judging by the looks of him. I just don't get it.

Now I'm not only lonely for Dad; I'm also desperately lonely for my friends. I feel cut off from everything, and, despite myself, I'm curious about what's happening with the Gotcha game. I can see who is still in the game by checking Facebook, but I want to hear the stories. I consider calling Mariah after school to get some news. If she's not with Paige, she might be willing to talk to me. And besides, we have to finish our project on the Tlingit. Maybe I can ask her to bring me some books.

The day drags on, but finally it's three o'clock. I dial Mariah's number.

"Hey, 'Riah, it's me, Katie," I say when she picks up the phone.

"Katie! How are you?" she asks, sounding genuinely interested. "I've missed you!"

"I've missed you too. Are you alone? Can you talk?"

"Yeah, I am. How's your ankle?"

"It's a little better. I think I'll be back at school next week. If I wrap it up tight, I may be able to walk around a bit."

"That's good."

"Yeah."

There's an awkward pause. I don't know what to say next. Clearly she doesn't either.

"So, how are Paige and Tanysha?"

"They're okay, but Tanysha lost her bead."

"No way! How?"

"It was so random," she says. "Paige's mom picked both of them up after their choir practice on Tuesday night. She drove right up Tanysha's driveway to the door, thinking that would be completely safe, but it was dark, so no one saw

Brent Taylor crouching behind a bush right beside the house."

"Oh no."

"Oh yes."

"How about Paige?"

"She's still got hers. But…" Mariah pauses.

"What?"

"She's acting…weird, like she's totally traumatized by the whole thing. Apparently she just kept screaming and screaming when she saw Tanysha get tagged, like she'd witnessed a shooting or something."

"Yeah, well, she's always been strung a little too tight," I say, and regret it immediately, but Mariah just laughs.

"She's been twice as bad since you guys had your fight, a real grouch."

I think about that. "Do you think I should try apologizing again?"

Mariah pauses before she answers. "I don't know, Katie. I'd say she owes you an apology for what she started at Tyson's."

Just talking about the game is bringing me down again. "Gotcha is bad news for everyone," I say.

"Tell me about it. Only one person wins, but in the meantime all kinds of people start hating each other. Did you hear about the Reynolds family?"

"No. What?"

"Well, Corrine never got around to telling her dad that we're playing Gotcha, but her brother, Craig, knew.

When Travis showed up at her house, her dad let him in, even though Craig was right there and could have said something. Travis tagged Corrine, so she is totally pissed at her dad, who is pissed at Craig for not telling him about the game. Craig thought the whole thing was a big joke, which ticked Corrine off even more. Now they're all fighting, and her mom even went to the school to complain about the game."

"Oh-oh."

"Yeah. A grade twelve meeting has been called for tomorrow afternoon. Rumor has it that Fetterly is going to try to shut us down. He'll probably threaten to suspend anyone who's caught playing."

"Are you serious?"

"That's what everyone's saying."

"Do you think that will be enough to make everyone quit?" My stomach clenches. I've just loaned my dad all the Gotcha money.

"Are you kidding? Not a chance! People will just get quieter about it."

Quieter about it. Great. It will just get more sinister than ever. But at least I won't be asked to return the money. I'd have some explaining to do about that.

"Maybe I should be at that meeting."

"It's up to you. If you don't make it, I'll come over and tell you what's going on."

"Thanks, 'Riah. But won't Paige be ticked if you come to see me?"

"Believe me, Katie, I really don't care. She's like totally weirded-out right now."

I know that is a giant leap for Mariah.

"How's your section of the Tlingit project going?" I ask.

"I'm done!" she says. "Can you believe it?"

I can't, really. I figured I'd be doing more than my share, as usual. "That's great. Maybe you can give me your portion at school tomorrow, I'll write a conclusion and then we can turn it in next week."

"Perfect."

"Hey, how's Jefferson?"

"He is like *so* amazing," she gushes. "And we're official. Did you hear?"

"No! That's so cool, Mariah. At least one good thing came out of this stupid game."

"You wouldn't believe it, Katie. He's so sweet, and he treats me like I'm…I'm special. I've never met a guy like him before."

I could point out that she's only been interested in creeps in the past, but then I remember that it's best to keep my mouth shut. And maybe it's Jefferson who's giving her the confidence to stand up to Paige. And to get her schoolwork done. All the power to him if that's the case. I love hearing her sound so happy.

"Hey, have you seen Joel?" she asks.

"Joel Keister?" Like there's any other Joel in our class.

"Yeah."

"Not since Tyson's party."

"He asked me about you."

"He did?" Stay calm, oh fluttering heart.

"Yeah. He said he was worried about you but didn't know what to say."

"Are you serious?"

"Uh-huh. He looked so sad, like a puppy dog in trouble."

"Maybe I should call him."

"You really should."

"It's just that…well, I must have looked so lame lying there on the floor that night. And those people trying to tear us apart. I felt like such an idiot."

"That was a crazy scene. I didn't know what to do. I wanted to help you, but if I'd tried…well, you know."

I know, and yet I don't. She'd had to choose between Paige and me. Maybe half the people at the party that night had felt like Mariah did and really didn't want to participate in the mobbing. What if they'd spoken up? Would Tyson and his friends have backed off? Or would they have turned on those who came to our defense? It seemed like they all became possessed by that stupid crowd mentality at the same time and really didn't stop to consider what they were doing. I've been to games—basketball and hockey—where the crowd seems to think it's a matter of life and death that the home team wins, and when there's a fight they become crazed gladiators. These were probably normal people when they arrived, but the energy created by the crowd seems to overwhelm even the most decent people.

"Gotcha makes everything weird, 'Riah. I don't know what I'd have done if it had been someone else getting picked on that night." I know what I like to think I would have done, but would I? Look what happened to Joel for defending me. "I think I'll give Joel a call right now. I owe him an apology."

"You should. He's almost as sweet as Jefferson."

Sweeter, I think but don't say. "Thanks for talking to me, Mariah. I've been going crazy all week."

"I should have called you. I will call tomorrow if I don't see you at the meeting."

"Say hi to Jefferson for me."

"I will." I can picture her smiling as she hangs up.

I put down the phone and sit back, savoring the warm glow that is spreading over me like a blush. Joel asked about me! I know that it's not a big deal and I shouldn't read anything into it and he is just a guy, but still. I wonder why he didn't just call? He must have known I was upset when I got home on Saturday night, and that's why I pushed him away. He didn't really think I blamed him for what happened, did he?

I find his phone number in the directory, but I just can't bring myself to dial the number. My dad's bizarre behavior this morning was enough rejection for one day. I don't think I could handle any more. And yet, as I stare at the phone, longing to talk to him, I remember those laughing eyes and his arm warm against mine. The palm of his hand was soft where it pressed into the back of mine on the crutch handle.

His loud bursts of laughter always made me laugh, even when I didn't know what was funny.

I'm so lost in Joel thoughts that I just about launch out of my chair when the phone rings. I grab the receiver and tell my heart to settle down. "Hello?"

"Katie?"

I can't believe it. It's Joel. Did I telepathically will him to call me?

"Yeah, it's me. That's weird. I was just thinking about you."

"You were? Good thoughts?"

I smile. "Of course."

"I was just talking to Mariah on MSN, and she suggested I call you."

Oh. So much for telepathy.

"She must have told you we were just talking on the phone."

"Yeah, she mentioned it."

So he's not calling because he wants to, but because Mariah told him to. My initial elation at hearing his voice evaporates.

"How's your ankle?" he asks.

"A little better. I'm starting to put some weight on it."

"That's good."

"Yeah."

There's a long pause. "How are *you*?" I ask finally.

"I'm okay." I hear him inhaling a deep breath. Then he lets it out. "Katie, I was really upset about what happened the other night. I felt so bad, and responsible. Are you still mad?"

"Of course not!" So that was it. He really did believe that he was responsible. "I told you it wasn't your fault. The whole game is stupid, and I even told Warren I was quitting."

"You did?"

"Yep."

"What did he say?"

"He said I couldn't. That it was against the rules."

Joel laughs at the absurdity of it. "Really?"

"Yeah, so I told him that in that case, I was just going to let myself get tagged. It would amount to the same thing."

"What did he say to that?"

"There wasn't much he could say."

"But you haven't done it."

"No, but only because I can't get myself to school." As soon as the words are out of my mouth, I realize how lame I sound. I could have stood at the end of my driveway. It wouldn't have taken long for word to get out that I wanted to get rid of my bead. Maybe I don't really want out as badly as I'd claimed.

"Well I'm glad you didn't," Joel says.

"Why?"

"'Cause think how ticked they'll all be if you win in the end."

"Yeah, that would show them, wouldn't it?" I smile at the thought and then consider telling Joel that, in my own way, I am going to come out the winner anyway after Dad invests the Gotcha money. But something cautions me against telling anyone about that just yet. Even Joel.

"'Riah said there's rumors going around that the game might get shut down anyway."

"That won't happen. But the rumors have ramped up everyone's efforts to get out there and get their bead sooner rather than later. Even I'm about to jump into the game. I was thinking of going hunting right now. Want to come along?"

"Hunting?"

"Yeah, bead-hunting. I've got my mom's car. We'll drive around, check out the usual hangouts. Who knows? We may get lucky."

"I don't know…"

"See? You are still mad."

"I am not!"

"If you weren't mad, you'd come with me."

"It's just that I'm not very mobile yet, so what's the point? I won't be able to chase anyone down. And besides, I still haven't decided whether I'm going to play this stupid game. I lost interest last weekend." Actually, I never had much interest in the first place.

"Okay, fine. But how about coming along and keeping me company and being there if I need to link to someone."

"Ohhh! You just want me along to keep you safe. I'd say you're using me. It's all about you, isn't it, Paige, I mean Joel," I tease.

Joel bursts out laughing but then goes back to pleading. "C'mon, Katie, we'll have fun. We'll grab some dinner and make a whole evening of it."

"What's in it for me?"

"You get to hang with me. What could be better than that?"

Now it's my turn to laugh. "It doesn't get much more Paige-like than that!"

"Please?" Joel begs.

"Okay, already, how soon are you going to be here?"

"Yeah, Katie! I'll be there in forty-five minutes. And you should wear black."

"Yes, sir."

"And do you have any binoculars?"

"Yes. Are we going bird-watching?"

Joel ignores me. "How about walkie-talkies? They might come in handy too."

"Sorry, no walkie-talkies."

"No problem."

"I'll be ready."

"And Katie?"

"Yeah?"

"I'm so glad you're not mad at me."

I smile and hang up the phone.

Eight

"Where should we go?" Joel asks, backing his mom's Subaru out of our driveway.

It's like there never was any misunderstanding between us. Joel arrived, all smiles, helped me into the car, and the anguish of the week is already melting away. I sit back and sigh. "I dunno. Anywhere. It just feels so good to get out of the house. It's been days."

"Aha! You wanted to get out after all, and yet you still made me beg."

I feel myself blush. "It's the bead-hunting I'm not so crazy about. Getting out is all good."

Joel smiles and turns down our street, heading toward the town center. I don't bother mentioning that I actually was out earlier today, with my dad, because that doesn't count. I wasn't feeling good about that outing.

We spend the first half hour of our bead-hunting adventure just driving around aimlessly. The car doors are locked and the windows are rolled up, for safety. Nothing would surprise me right now, not even someone running over to the car at a stoplight and hopping in to tag one of us.

The town is busy with people shopping and parents driving kids to their activities, but I don't spot any other grads. It is nice to be out, but driving without a destination eventually grows dull.

"How 'bout we get a coffee?" I suggest.

"We could," Joel says, glancing at me, "but I don't want to run into a coffee shop alone, and it might be a little awkward trying to carry coffee, linked, and with you on crutches."

Clearly I'm not thinking like a good bead-hunter. "Then how about a drive-through place? Do you know one that makes good lattes?"

Joel checks his rearview mirror and pulls into the right lane. "I do, actually."

A few minutes later we're sitting in the parking lot of a strip mall, sipping hot drinks out of paper cups.

"So what Gotcha excitement have I missed this week?"

"Oh man," Joel says. "Where to start?"

"Anywhere."

"Well, let's see. Did you hear about Sam?"

"No, what?"

Joel shakes his head. "He's really blown it." Sam is another classmate who we've gone to school with since first grade.

"What did he do?"

"Well, you know how he and Mike are—or were—like, really close?"

"Yeah. Like pretty much inseparable."

"Exactly. And you know how Mike was totally into Gotcha?"

"Totally? Like worse than everyone else? Even Tyson?"

"Yeah, if you can believe it."

"That's hard to believe, but okay."

"So Sam phones him up and suggests they hit a bucket of balls or something. They're always doing stuff like that together."

I turn in my seat to face Joel, wondering where he's going with this.

"Sam arrives at Mike's in his car to pick him up, and Mike jumps into the front seat. What Mike doesn't know is that Joanie is ducking down in the backseat. As soon as he pulls the door shut, she sits up, reaches over the seat and tags him."

"Sam set him up?" I can't believe it! Sam and Mike have been friends forever.

"Sam set him up. And Mike is pissed."

"How did Sam justify it?"

"He said it's a game. No big deal. Everyone's in it for themselves."

"Hmm."

"But now Mike is helping Carl, who has Sam's name, and Mike's seriously out for revenge."

I nod. It's one thing to tag your friend if you have their name, but to set them up? I don't think I'd do that to Paige, even though our friendship has been pretty sketchy lately.

"And then there was the TJ and Jamie episode."

"What happened with them?"

Joel takes the last sip of his latte and squashes the paper cup. "Jamie has TJ's name. He knows TJ usually gets off work at the restaurant around nine, so he's crouching in some bushes right by TJ's car, waiting to tag him. Only trouble is, TJ doesn't end up getting off work until eleven. Jamie's still squatting in the bushes, freezing his butt off, when TJ comes out of the restaurant. He tries to leap up and tag TJ, but his muscles have all seized up from squatting so long."

I laugh, picturing it.

Joel is smiling too. "TJ sees this guy stumbling out of the bushes toward him, so he throws off his backpack and sprints away. With his stiff muscles, Jamie hasn't got a hope of catching up, but he does grab the backpack. Turns out TJ's paycheck is in there. Two hundred dollars worth of paycheck."

"Whoa! Nice."

"Yeah. So Jamie phones up TJ the next day and tells him if he wants his money, he has to come and get the backpack."

"Kinda like ransom."

"Kinda like." Joel nods. "But TJ's no dummy. He knows if he collects the backpack he'll get tagged and give up all hope of winning the two-thousand-plus Gotcha prize. So he forfeits the paycheck, figuring he'll still be a couple of thousand dollars richer if he wins the game."

"Omigod." I sink back in my seat. "This is crazy."

"I know."

I think about these stories for a minute. "Has Tyson still got his beads?" I ask.

"I think so. Why?"

"I figure he's got my name. That's why he tried to get me to unlink from you at the party."

"Or maybe he has my name."

"Yeah. Could be."

"One strategy people are using to get beads is to tell their victim, in a Gotcha-free zone like school, that they know who has their name. After the person begs and pleads to be told who it is, the bead snatcher pretends to give in and then tells them any random name, just to throw them off-track. That way, the person is not cautious around the real bead snatcher, and they become easier targets."

"Has that worked for anyone?"

"Oh yeah. Quite a few beads were lost that way at the start, but now everyone's becoming too bead savvy."

"Bead savvy?"

"Yeah." He smiles. "There's a whole new lingo springing up too."

"I've noticed. Bead hunting, bead savvy, bead season."

"Gotcha-free zone."

"Bead crazy. Bead snatcher."

"Unlink. And then there's the bead cheaters."

"Bead cheaters?" I smile. "How do they get away with cheating?"

"There's a few ways. One is for two people to work together. They start telling someone else conflicting stories about who has that person's name. Because that person is confused, any one of a number of people could tag them, and they wouldn't know that their name had actually changed hands a few times."

"How does that work? Only one person wins."

"I'm not really sure, but I guess they have a plan to split the prize money or something. I wouldn't trust anyone at this point."

"Even me?"

He looks at me and grins. My stomach flip-flops. "I think I could trust you, but only because you've been cooped up too long and don't know the ins and outs of the game very well."

I punch his arm. "Are you calling me bead un-savvy?"

"Maybe just a little bead naïve."

I have to laugh, and it feels good. "So," I say, looking around the parking lot, "there doesn't seem to be a lot of bead action happening here."

"Ahh. Bead action. Another new term coined. Maybe we could compile a manual."

"Yeah." I consider it. "We could sell it to next year's grads, to give them a *bead-up* on the game, so to speak."

Joel's eyes shine. "We could list rules and strategies, and write out urban legends from Gotcha games in years gone by."

"Hmm. Maybe not, Joel," I say, thinking of something Warren mentioned in our telephone conversation. "I think part of the mystique of the game is that nothing is written down. The rules and stories have been handed down by word of mouth forever."

Joel gives me a curious look.

"Okay, maybe not forever, but for many years, anyway. Who knows, it may go on to become generations."

"Oh my God," Joel says.

"You're right. Who'd wish this on their kids?"

The parking lot has been quiet, but now a car pulls in to the stall right next to ours. The booming of its stereo makes the windows of Joel's car vibrate.

"Speak of the devil," Joel says, leaning over to link arms with me.

I peer into the tinted windows of the next car and see Tyson in the driver's seat. Troy is in the passenger seat, and I can see three bodies in the back, though I can't tell who they are. My stomach knots at the sight of Tyson. The vision of his crazy dance with my crutch at the party is still fresh in my mind.

Tyson rolls down his window and motions for me to do the same thing.

I glance at Joel. "Go for it," he says, giving my arm a squeeze.

"So look who's back in action," Tyson says once my window is down. He grins at me. The guy looks possessed. He really does. His eyes gleam in an unnatural way, and he holds up his wrist so I can see the four beads dangling from his bracelet. "Bead-hunting tonight?" he asks, looking past me to Joel.

Joel shrugs. "Just hanging."

Tyson laughs. "Yeah, right."

Troy leans over Tyson from the passenger seat and holds up his arm for us to see the three beads strung on his wristband. "Just got my third one," he yells over the music.

"Yeah, and was it ever sweet," Tyson says. He and Troy slap hands and then Troy slaps hands with each of the three guys in the backseat.

"What happened?" Joel asks.

Tyson begins to tell us but then realizes we can't hear a thing over his music. He hits the power button on his stereo and turns to say something to the guys in the rear. They all pile out through the back door and lumber off toward the coffee shop, safely linked. Tyson and Troy have also emerged through the front door, and they lean against Tyson's car, trying to look relaxed. I'm tempted to whip open my door and pin Tyson to his car with it, but somehow I restrain myself.

"So, we were just cruising around," Troy tells us, eyes shining, "when we see Rebecca in her car, and she's got Josie and Merle with her."

"Troy had Josie's name," Tyson says.

"Yeah, and we knew Merle had Justin's name," Troy adds, naming one of the guys who has just gone off for coffee.

"So we followed them around for a while, but it got boring," Tyson says. "We knew they weren't going to take any chances, and neither were we."

"That's when I got this brilliant idea," Troy says. "I got Justin to switch his ballcap and jacket with me. We also traded seats in the car when we knew they couldn't see us."

Tyson takes over the storytelling. "So I pulled in to a parking stall by a gas station with a convenience store. We wait for the girls to pull up near us because we want them to see us get out of the car. We link up and go into the store."

"Justin and I keep our heads down so they don't realize the switch we've made," Troy adds.

"The girls just hover around outside the door of the store," Tyson says, "spying on us. That's when Troy makes his move. He unlinks from me, supposedly just long enough to pull out his wallet to pay for his Slurpee. Merle thinks he's Justin, so she unlinks from Josie and books it into the store to tag him, but Justin turns out to be Troy."

"You should have seen Merle's face when she realized she'd been had," Troy says, laughing. "What a joke!"

"Troy then sees that Josie is standing alone," Tyson continues. "Rebecca, being the flake she is, has moved a few feet away and is distracted by some guy at one of the gas pumps. He's talking to her, and she's probably admiring his muscles or something, so she doesn't see what's going down. Before Josie can get hooked up with her again, Troy runs out of the store, toward Josie. She screams, and races down the street, but Troy is too fast."

Troy holds up his arm to admire his beads. "And isn't it lovely."

"Did Merle ever get Justin's bead?" I ask.

"Nope. He's still in."

Too bad, I think.

"So whose name do you have now?" Joel asks Troy, all innocence.

"Like I'm going to tell you, Keister!" Troy laughs. "Nice try."

The three stooges have returned with paper cups. They slide into the backseat of Tyson's car.

"Rumor has it you might be giving your bead away," Tyson says to me.

I shrug and feign interest in a seagull that's rummaging through some dumped garbage. I'm certainly not sharing anything with him.

"Well then," he says, "I guess we'll be seeing you around. Glad you've found the balls to leave your house again," he adds, smirking.

Now I wish I had slammed him with my car door.

Troy gets into Tyson's car through the driver's door and slides across to the passenger seat. Tyson follows, somehow managing to remain linked the whole time, which makes me think that he suspects one of us of having his name. He puts the keys in the ignition, hits the power on the stereo and they squeal away.

"This game exposes a person's true colors, doesn't it?" Joel comments, unraveling his arm from mine. I'm glad to see Tyson leave, but disappointed to lose the physical connection with Joel.

"Yeah."

We resume driving around, without direction, but the carefree mood of the afternoon has evaporated. Tyson has really gotten to me. Did he actually believe I stayed home all week because I was scared? Jerk. And something else is gnawing at the back of my mind too. There's something about the Gotcha stories that bothers me. It takes me a moment to put my finger on it, but eventually it dawns on me.

"Have more girls than boys lost their beads?" I ask Joel.

He tilts his head, considering it. "I don't know. We'd have to check Facebook. But it does seem like it, doesn't it?"

"Yeah, it does."

I'm now realizing that all this driving is pointless, and I'm wondering why Joel even suggested it in the first place.

"So what were the binoculars for?" I ask.

"For spying on your victim."

"And the black clothes?" The answer is obvious, but I figure I'll ask anyway.

"For the same reason cat burglars and prowlers wear black. To blend in with the night."

I shake my head. "You're a nutbar."

He smiles. "Might as well make it fun. It's supposed to be a game."

His answer startles me. At what point did I forget that? Come to think of it, did I ever know it was supposed to be fun?

"But it's not even dark," I tell him.

"It will be, later."

"You think I'm still going to be driving around here with you later?"

"If I don't take you home you will be."

"So we're doing this to have fun." I'm still trying to get my head around that.

He glances at me, puzzled. "Why else would we be doing it?"

He's right. Why else? "For the money, I guess."

"Yeah, I guess that's another good reason."

"You realize that this isn't the most intelligent way of stalking your victim, don't you?"

"No?" he asks, teasing. "So how would you go about it?"

"I'd do research on them. Find out what their habits are. Where they're likely to be at any given time."

Joel glances at me. "And have you done that?"

The question surprises me. I haven't. I've hardly given any thought to how I'm going to capture my first bead. "No."

Joel laughs. "So your strategy isn't working any better than mine."

I slap his arm, but I laugh too. "I guess if we want to get in the game, we better start doing some research."

"How about we discuss it over dinner?" he suggests.

"Good call," I say, pretending that having dinner with a guy is something I do all the time.

We decide to take the bridge across the river to the next town, hoping to find a place to eat without the constant fear of being tagged. After forty-five minutes of negotiating winding back roads, we find a diner that looks like a place no one but locals would hang out at. The décor is early seventies, with Arborite tabletops and an ancient jukebox squatting in a corner. The vinyl booth benches are slashed, and the stuffing is sprouting out in tufts. The only other people in the place are an old couple who are sitting in a booth by the window. The waitress motions for us to take the one across from them. I hobble over and slide onto the bench. Joel takes my crutches and lays them on the floor beside the table.

After studying the grimy plastic menu, Joel decides on a hamburger, and I order fish and chips.

"So," Joel says, running his fingers along the side of his water glass, wiping the condensation off, "in order to do research on our victims, I guess we're going to have to tell each other who we're stalking."

I study his face, sizing him up. "I don't know about that."

"How else will we be able to help each other?"

"You said yourself that we can't trust anyone."

"I wasn't talking about me!" Joel tries to look insulted, but, as usual, his eyes give him away. I realize that he really is having fun with this game.

Maybe it's nerves, or maybe it's exasperation, but something inside me snaps. I suddenly feel crazily defiant. "I've just decided something," I tell Joel.

"And what is that?"

"That I absolutely have to win this stupid game." The conviction of my words surges through me as I say them out loud. I sit up straighter. "I need the money, and it would be the perfect way to get back at Tyson." It would be! I like what I'm hearing myself say. "And besides, it bugs me that the guys seem to be getting all the beads. It has to be a girl that wins."

Where did that come from? I just opened my mouth and the words came rushing out.

Joel looks puzzled. "Okay, but what's that got to do with trusting me?"

"I can't trust anyone if I'm going to win. Haven't you ever watched *Survivor*?"

Joel laughs so hard and loud that the old couple at the booth across from us turn their heads and glare at him.

"So why do you need the money so bad?" he asks, whispering sheepishly, his eyes shining again.

"So I can go to college next year."

"There's always scholarships, and student loans. And you have a job." He's stopped whispering, but his voice is low.

"But you never know for sure whether you're going to win the scholarships or get the loans. The Gotcha money would be a sure thing. It would at least get me started. And I've really got to move out of my house."

His eyes soften a little. "What's happening at home?"

I have no intention of telling him anything. It's none of his business. But my mouth opens and more words just burble out. "My dad left us, and my mom makes me crazy."

"Oh." He looks surprised. "I think your mom is sweet."

"No. You think she makes good cookies."

"That too." He smiles.

My God, he has a beautiful smile. I have to take a deep breath.

"Anyway," he says, "winning works for me. We work together, and if we win we split the money fifty-fifty."

"When we win," I tell him. "Not if."

"Of course. When." The laugh lines deepen again.

"That's what Paige wanted me to do," I tell him. "Team up with her and split the winnings, but I wouldn't."

"I wouldn't team up with Paige either. She hasn't proven herself worthy. But c'mon, Katie, I'm good. We can do this."

"You're good?"

"Yeah."

"Good at what?"

"Well, I'm still in the game, for one thing."

"So is Paige."

"Okay, so that wasn't a great example." He takes a sip of his water while he thinks about it. He sits up straighter. "Don't forget, Katie, that I stuck with you at that stupid Gotcha party. I wouldn't have released your arm for anything, even if they had promised me bead immunity."

"Bead immunity?" Now it's my turn to laugh. I can feel the old people glaring at me. "Omigod, Joel. Don't let me forget to put that one in the Gotcha game manual."

"I won't." He turns to the elderly couple. "I'll make her settle down," he assures them. "She tends to get a little carried away." Then he turns to me and puts his fingers to his lips. With my good foot, I kick him under the table. He just smiles in return.

The waitress slides two plates onto the table and we eat quietly for a moment. The old couple lose interest in us and go back to their own meals.

I consider the idea of sharing the names of our victims. Would he really be able to help me?

"Why would you pair up with me, Joel? These crutches seriously cramp my style. You'd be better off with just about anyone else."

Joel doesn't answer for a few seconds. When he does, he looks directly at me. "Because it would be fun. And it would give us a chance to hang out together more."

Did he really just say what I think I just heard? I know it's not a confession of undying love, but I'm struck dumb anyway. Why would a guy like Joel want to hang with me? I look down at my plate and concentrate on stabbing a French fry with my fork. The mood at our table has flipped 180 degrees with just those few words. I hope my face isn't as red as it feels.

"Sorry, Katie," he says, putting his burger down and wiping his hands on a napkin. "I didn't mean to embarrass you."

I glance back up and see that he's blushing too. I go back to concentrating on my French fries.

"It's just that we always have fun together," he says.

I know what I should say. I know what I want to say. But the words just won't come out. Why is it so much easier for me to say hurtful things than nice things?

"Forget I brought it up," he says and goes back to eating his hamburger.

I keep on stabbing French fries, but I don't bring them to my mouth. I realize I've done it again. I've pushed him away, and for no good reason. What is the matter with me?

The silence that follows is awkward. I rack my brain for something I can talk about, something to ask him, but my mind is blank. A few minutes ago, words were just tumbling out of my mouth. Now there's nothing. Where did they all go? Joel finishes his burger and pushes his plate away. We watch as the old couple in the booth across the way struggle out of their seats and shuffle to the door.

The waitress comes to remove our plates and asks if we want any dessert. Joel says no thanks and looks to me for my answer. Our eyes meet and I see that he's trying to mask whatever it is he's feeling. There are no laugh lines visible now. I shake my head at the waitress and she leaves. The silence at our table is a roar in my ears.

"Have you got a pen?" I ask Joel.

"Huh?"

"A pen."

He shakes his head, but the waitress is back with our bill. "Can I borrow your pen for a minute?" I ask her.

She yanks one out of her apron and drops it on the table beside the bill.

I pick it up and pull a napkin out of the dispenser on the table. I tear a corner off the napkin and jot a name on it. Then I fold the scrap of napkin four times. I push it across the table to Joel.

His eyebrows arch. "What's this?" he asks.

"The name of my victim," I tell him.

"And you're giving it to me because…?"

"Because I want us to be a team."

"Are you sure?" He looks like he's afraid to believe it.

"I'm sure."

He just stares at the scrap. I reach over, pick it up and push it into his palm. Using both hands, I close his fingers around it. "Read it," I tell him. "I want you to." I push his hand away.

He opens his hand, stares at the note for a moment and then places it, still folded, on the table. The next thing I know, he's reached across the table for my hands and encloses them with both of his. "Did I pressure you into this, Katie? I know I can be overenthusiastic—that's how we got into trouble at the party. We don't have to share names if you don't want to. I'm okay with that. Honest."

My hands feel so small in his large ones, but warm and protected too. I can only look back at him and nod.

"You're sure."

"I am," I laugh. "Totally sure. I don't know why I didn't say so in the first place. I think I was just…nervous. I'm not used to…"

"What?"

"I don't know."

"C'mon. What were you going to say?"

"Guys. Guy friends. I don't have many." There. The truth is on the table.

"Why not?" He looks genuinely surprised.

"I don't know. Paige says I scare them off."

Joel throws his head back and laughs again. It's a good thing the old people have left. The noise of it might have given them heart attacks. I figure it's a compliment, in a warped sort of way.

Joel grabs the pen and rips off his own scrap of napkin. He writes something on it, folds it up and pushes it across the table to me. "That's the name of my victim," he says.

I smile. "So, what do we do? Say, one, two, three, open?"

"Might as well," Joel says.

"Okay then." We each put a scrap directly in front of us. "One...two...hang on!" I say, just as Joel is reaching for the one I passed him.

"What's wrong?" he asks.

"What if you just scribbled some nonsense on yours, and I gave you the real thing?"

"Would I do that?" He acts totally offended.

"I don't know, Joel. Maybe you would. How well do I really know you?"

He regards me seriously. "About as well as I know you. Maybe you just scribbled something on yours to drag a name out of me. Maybe someone has bribed you to set me up. What do any of us know for sure?"

His eyes are in full-laugh mode.

"Ohmigod. If you've tricked me, Mr. Keister...you will never..."

"I will never what?" he challenges.

"You will never..." I have no idea what to threaten him with. "You will never win, I'll make damn sure of that!"

"One, two, three, open!" he says. I grab the scrap of paper and unfold it quickly. I read the name he has written on it. Our eyes meet. Joel grins, but I have to look away. Suddenly everything becomes crystal clear, and my heart sinks completely.

Nine

"I can't help you with this," I tell Joel and push the scrap of paper back across the table. My eyes are burning, but I can't let him see that.

"Why not?"

Because you're an ass and you're only using me to get to her and I can't believe I actually thought there was something else going on here.

"Because she's my friend," I tell him, deciding there's no need to spell out the obvious. "I can't set up my best friend."

"But it's just a game, Katie, remember?"

"Maybe, but I know for sure that Paige would never again be my friend if I helped you tag her."

"Did she act like your friend at Tyson's party?"

"No. But…"

"But what?"

"That was different."

"How?"

"She didn't actually set up the mobbing. It wasn't intentional. She just didn't stop it once it started." Why am

I getting into this argument with him? It's all irrelevant now anyway.

"It seems about the same to me."

I shrug and dig through my purse, looking for my wallet so I can get money to pay for my dinner.

"And I'm going to help you get Warren," Joel says. "You might as well start counting out the Gotcha cash now, half for you, half for me."

I guess it's the way he's talking, like he thinks I can't figure out why he's hooked up with me, but it all becomes too much and finally I snap. "You must think I'm a real idiot, Joel. I don't know why I didn't figure it out before now."

Joel looks genuinely puzzled. He'd make a fine actor.

"You never knew I existed until Gotcha started," I tell him, "and then suddenly you're my best buddy. I can't believe I didn't figure it out."

"Figure what out?"

I stare at him. Is he serious? "That you have the name of one of my friends!"

Joel slumps back in the booth, another good acting job. This time he's portraying bewilderment. "You think that's what's happening here?" he asks.

"Well, duh," I tell him and slap my money on the table. I slide across the bench and reach for my crutches, but Joel beats me to them. He snatches them up and holds them out of my reach.

"I thought we understood each other," he says.

"Oh yeah, I understand you now," I say, swinging my arm out to grab back the crutches.

"You've got it all wrong," Joel says, still holding them behind him.

"Right." I stare him down. "You expect me to believe that you haven't befriended me strictly to get Paige's bead?"

"No I have not," he says, looking directly back at me. Gone are any trace of laugh lines, and he looks steamed.

"You've got to admit," I say. "It looks pretty suspicious."

He nods. "I guess it does. But it never occurred to me that you'd think I was using you to get to Paige. It is just a coincidence for me that I've become...acquainted with my victim's friend."

He looks so sincere, and I feel myself begin to soften, but then I realize how stupid that would be. I force myself to see past the sparkling eyes, the dazzling smile, the easy-going attitude. "You said yourself that you can't trust anyone in this game," I remind him. "And that it is 'just' a game. And that anything goes. So what am I supposed to think?"

Joel runs a hand through his hair, thinking. "Sit down, Katie," he says, motioning to the bench.

I do, and he lays the crutches back down. I can see from the corner of my eye that the waitress is watching us. She's probably wishing we'd leave so she can lock the place up.

"You never showed any interest in being my friend until Gotcha began," I say.

"That's true. We didn't know each other. But that night you came to rescue Paige from Elijah's house, well, it reminded me of the crush I'd had on you when we were little kids."

"Right."

"And I kept thinking about you," he says, ignoring my sarcasm. He speaks softly, earnestly. "So I decided to ask you to Tyson's party, just because I wanted to hang together, not because of Gotcha or Paige."

How I wish I could believe him.

"Hey," he says, suddenly looking up. "Did I look one bit concerned when I heard you'd had a fight with Paige?"

"I don't remember."

"Well if this had been about me using you to get to Paige, that would have been a serious problem for me. But I didn't care. And we did have fun at that party until…"

"Whatever, Joel," I say. "I still can't help you tag Paige. That would be a definite friendship-ender." Not that I really care at the moment, but still. I have principles.

We sit in awkward silence. Joel's finger taps the edge of his glass. "I'm going to prove to you that I didn't befriend you just to get Paige's bead," he says finally, leaning into the table.

"And how are you going to do that?" I ask.

"I'm not sure yet," he says. "But I'm working on it."

I can sense that he's studying my face, but I can't make eye contact with him. Suddenly he stands up, leans right across the table and kisses me, softly. I should push him away, or lean back where he can't reach me, but I don't.

I hear the waitress clear her throat. Joel must have heard her too, because he sits back on his bench. "Is that proof enough?" he asks.

"It proves nothing," I tell him. Except that his lips felt wonderful on mine, warm, soft, even if it was such a brief connection.

"Well then, I guess I have to help you tag Warren first."

I nod. My cheeks are burning.

"He's got quite a few beads, by the way."

"Really?" I should care, but somehow I don't. I only care that I've just been kissed, by Joel.

Joel leans forward and whispers, "You look especially pretty when you're blushing."

I groan and roll my eyes, but I can feel my face turning redder still. He yanks his wallet out of the pocket of his jeans and digs through it for some money. "You know, Katie, I'd drop out of the game right now if it would make you believe that I'm not using you to win the game."

"Warren won't let you drop out," I remind him.

"Oh yeah," he says. "Good." He places his money on the table and grins. "Because it's just becoming interesting."

The kiss we share when we get back to my house is a little longer and warmer still, but I don't linger too long. I'm still wary of him. And so is my mom.

"Where have you been?" she demands as I hobble into the house.

"Out. I left a note on the counter."

"Just saying you're going 'out' is not good enough, Katie," she says. "I had no way of knowing where you were, what you were up to, who you were with. I was worried."

How stupid is that! I'll be gone, living on my own, in a few months. Her worrying is coming a few years too late. "I was out doing drugs and having unprotected sex," I snap back.

"Katie!" she says.

"Oh c'mon, Mom. You know me better than that. I was with Joel, discussing strategy for the Gotcha game. No big deal."

"Necking with a boy in the driveway, where all the neighbors can see you, is not discussing strategy."

"You were spying on me!"

"No, I just happened to look out the window, much like all the neighbors were probably doing."

"I can't believe this." I have never given her one moment of worry in all my high school years, and suddenly I'm a slut for getting a good-night kiss. Grad and college can't come soon enough.

I hobble past her and to the computer. I can feel her eyes on my back.

"There's nothing to worry about, Mom."

She sighs. "Just use some discretion in the future, Katie. Good night." I hear her trudge up the stairs. For one guilty second I wonder if she's lonely without Dad. But then I decide I don't care.

I check the group page on Facebook and, sure enough, Warren does have six beads. Bonus. The game appears to be down to forty-eight players. I count up the girls who are still left playing. Only ten. I was right. The boys have been playing harder for some reason. That's got to change.

I know I have to get back to school, and I'd really like to be at the grade twelve meeting tomorrow afternoon. I consider my options. I could phone Paige and ask how she's been getting to school and whether she'll go with me. But I really don't want to do that. Especially now.

And then there's Dad. He's still driving a car and doesn't appear to have anywhere to go during the day. Maybe he could behave like a father and get me to school.

From: kittiekat17@hotmail.com
To: dannyo56@hotmail.com
Subject: getting 2 school

hi dad, n e chance u could pick me up tm morning & drive me 2 school? It's 2 far 2 go on crutches, but im getting really far behind. i could use a ride home 2.

thnks,
Katie

I plunk myself in front of the TV for an hour, giving Dad a chance to respond, but he doesn't. I finally go to bed and try to think of something besides Joel, but it's hopeless.

The kiss is still too fresh in my mind. I toss and turn for hours.

I check my e-mail for a message from Dad in the morning. Still nothing. I'm going to have to phone Paige or stay home again. I stare at the phone and decide to go for it. Somehow I'm in the mood to take chances.

Paige's phone rings four times. I know they have call display, so I expect Paige has seen who is phoning them and is ignoring my call. I'm just about to hang up when her mom picks up.

"Hi, Katie," she says, clearly happy to hear from me. "Long time no see. How are you?"

There's something about her tone and her cheerfulness that makes me think she doesn't know anything about the situation between Paige and me.

"It has been a while," I agree. "I don't know if Paige told you, but I've injured my ankle and I'm on crutches."

"Oh no! Paige has been…very quiet, not telling me much about anything. What happened?"

"Just a little accident. No big deal. But I was wondering how she is getting to school. I've been stuck home all week…"

"Do you want a ride?" she asks. "That silly bead game has got Paige terrified, so I've been driving her each day. I'd be happy to pick you up too."

This is too easy. I don't even have to talk to Paige.

"That would be so great. How soon are you leaving?"

"We'll pick you up at eight thirty."

I hang up and smile to myself, but the moment passes quickly. Paige is going to be majorly ticked that I wangled myself a ride, and she'll let me have it...though she might pretend everything is okay in front of her mom. It should be an interesting six-minute journey.

I see them pull in to my driveway at exactly 8:30. Paige gets out of the car and jogs up the walkway, glancing over her shoulder. I open the door and force myself to look directly into her face. Her eyes are flat, almost hard. There's no hint of friendliness or even forgiveness there. Where is my old friend Paige? What has happened to her?

"Nice trick, Katie."

"I just need to get to school and..."

"Whatever. My mom doesn't have a clue about what's been going on, so don't say a word."

"I won't." I start clomping down the path behind her. "I don't suppose you want to swap apologies?" I say to her back, just before we get to the car.

She turns to glare at me. "I haven't done anything to apologize for."

"Well I'm willing to apologize," I tell her. "And I'll try to forget what happened at Tyson's."

"We'll talk later," she mumbles and opens the back door for me. I slide across the seat and pull my crutches in behind me.

I'd forgotten how much alike Paige and her mother are—or used to be, before Gotcha started. Paige's mom babbles nonstop, unaware of Paige's black mood. When we get to the school, Paige waits while I climb out of the car and she watches her mom drive away. Then she turns and glares at me. "Our friendship can never be the same, Katie," she says, her voice dripping with bitterness. "You called me needy and attention-seeking. From now on, anytime I ever do anything, I'll wonder if you're thinking I'm seeking attention again. I can't live with that." She turns and starts marching toward the school.

My initial reaction is shock. I've always been honest with her. Why is she being so oversensitive this time? "Hey, Paige," I yell at her back. She swings around and stares at me. I ignore the steady stream of students who are emerging from their parents' cars and walking past us to the school.

"I never called you needy," I yell to her. "But I will say you're prone to exaggeration."

She stomps back to me, glancing nervously at anyone who may have heard my outburst.

"You could try a little harder to keep our conversation private," she says, her face right up to mine.

"Hey, you walked away without giving me a chance to speak," I say.

She looks around and crosses her arms. "Katie, best friends take each other just as they are and don't label them. I could call you a few unpleasant names too, you know."

"Go for it," I challenge her.

She thinks about that. "Okay. Let's start with know-it-all. Stuck-up. And frigid."

"That's the best you can do?" I ask, trying hard not to react to her words.

"Yeah, that's about it. But it stings, doesn't it?"

I nod. "Yeah, a little," I admit. "But not enough to give up on years of friendship."

"Then maybe I feel things deeper than you," she says.

"Maybe you do." Or maybe she's the ultimate drama queen. Or has an icy heart.

"So I can't be friends with you anymore," she reiterates.

"Okay." I shrug. "Although I find this very strange. I've always been honest with you, even when it hurts. But if that's the way it's got to be..."

She nods, not making eye contact with me.

"You know, there are other labels I could give you too, the ones that made me enjoy being your friend, even when you were attention-seeking."

Her eyes narrow. "Like what?"

"You used to be loveable. And funny. And spontaneous."

She glares at me.

"And at one time I would have called you loyal, too, but now I'm not so sure. Especially since Tyson's party."

The buzzer sounds for the start of first class.

"Goodbye, Katie," she says and walks off.

I sit through my classes, but I can't focus. Paige's labels for me are running through my mind, especially one. Frigid. Am I? Is that how Joel sees me?

I doodle in the back of my notebook while I examine my feelings. Being dumped by her has left me agitated but also relieved in some strange way. Being Paige's best friend was a lot of work, I realize. She's a bundle of insecurities, and I've always had to be strong for her and listen to her constant babble of unrelated thoughts. It was exhausting. I've seen her toss away other friends over the years, but I never thought she'd do it to me. There's something very odd about this. I was her anchor. She felt secure with me. She'd share her thoughts, sort out her feelings, realizing, all the while, that I knew she was simply "trying on" new ideas, and I wouldn't hold her to anything. And yet, did she do that for me?

I snap shut my notebook. Paige has always needed me more than I need her, and if she doesn't want to be friends, it's her loss.

At lunch break I hobble into the cafeteria and spot Paige sitting with Tanysha and Mariah at our usual table. Where will I sit? Just as I'm beginning to wish I'd stayed home again today, I feel a set of arms wrap around me from behind.

"You're here!" Joel says.

A warm glow spreads over me, yet I'm acutely aware that the noise in the cafeteria has dimmed, and I suspect that we're the cause of it. People aren't used to seeing me enclosed in a guy's arms. As nonchalantly as possible, I gently loosen his arms and turn to face him. The cafeteria chatter resumes. New relationships are always hot topics.

"It's so great to have you back at school," Joel says. He glances about, probably wondering why I'm red-faced. His gaze lingers on Paige's table, and he turns and regards me. "Problems?"

"Sort of."

While Joel considers the situation, I think about what it means that he hugged me in front of everyone. The nagging suspicion I still had that he was using me to get to Paige disappears. He's got to be for real.

"Do you want to get out of here?" he asks.

I nod and glance at Paige's table. All three of them are still staring at us. I turn and follow Joel back out of the cafeteria.

Just as we get through the doors, I hear my name being called. I swing around and find Mariah chasing after us.

"Hey," she says.

"Hey," I say back.

She nods back to the cafeteria. "Sorry about that. I didn't know what to do."

"That's okay. I understand."

"Jefferson's not here today...so I sat with them..."

"I'm serious, 'Riah. It's okay."

She shoves a folder of paper in my hand. "The Tlingit report," she says.

"Oh. Great," I say, taking it from her. "I'll finish it up on the weekend."

She just nods, but she's looking at me intently, like she really wants to say something.

"It's okay, Mariah. I understand. I really do."

I see her eyes well up just before she reaches out and pulls me into a hug. Then she turns and heads back to the cafeteria.

"Where's your lunch?" Joel asks when we're settled on the grass at the front of the school.

"It's too hard to make a sandwich while balancing on crutches," I tell him. "So I didn't bother today. But I'm okay."

"No you're not," he says. "Take this." He hands me half of his.

I want to refuse, but it looks so good, stacked high with ham, cheese and lettuce, that I take it. "Thanks."

"So," I say, after swallowing a large mouthful. "Paige officially dumped me as her friend this morning."

"Really?" Joel passes me his can of juice. "Are you okay?"

"Yeah, I am." I take a swig of his orange juice and pass it back. "I'm surprised, that's all. She always seemed to need me more than I needed her."

Joel nods.

"And I don't know where I stand with Tanysha. Mariah's cool. But I guess Tanysha and I were never all that close anyway. She's like a Paige groupie."

Joel rubs my back sympathetically. I wish he'd never stop. "You know what they say, Katie. When one door closes, another one always opens."

"Well aren't you the wise one," I tease. I look around the front yard of the school. "Funny, I don't see any doors opening."

Joel smiles. "Then you must be blind, Katie. A door has already swung wide open for you."

"It has? Where?"

"You're looking right at it," he says. He leans toward me and brushes his lips against mine. I wish he wouldn't stop.

"You're a door?"

He laughs, and a shivery rush of goose bumps breaks out on my arms. "I'm your new friend!" he tells me. "One walks out and another walks in."

"Oh, I get it."

He bumps his shoulder against mine. I lean into him and marvel at how easy he is to be with. So unlike Paige.

"I should warn you, Joel. Paige says I'm a know-it-all and stuck-up." I decide not to tell him she also called me frigid. No point putting notions in his head. "Maybe you should think about that before you get too friendly with me."

Joels taps his cheek with his finger. His eyes are narrowed, as if he is thinking really hard. "She's right," he says. "You are those things."

I push him away. "You're a bum."

He scoots back over. "I'm kidding!"

"Right."

Smiling, Joel passes me the juice can again, and when I hand it back, he takes the last sip, walks over to the school and tosses it in a recycling bin. He smacks hands with a friend, and I enjoy watching his easy gait as he returns to our spot on the lawn. Then he takes my hand in his.

"Thanks for not just tossing that can away," I say.

He looks at me, puzzled.

"That's what my old friend would have done, so I was always picking up after her." Now, I realize, she's tossed me away too.

"Sounds like you two were never the best match."

"No," I agree. "I guess we really weren't."

His hand squeezes mine.

"And I guess if Paige is no longer my friend, I'm free to help you get her bead."

Joel studies my face. "Are you okay with this?"

"Yeah, I am." I nod. And I'm going to enjoy seeing it happen, too.

Ten

Mr. Fetterly raises his hand, and the noise in the gym slowly subsides.

"Thank you all for coming today," he says. "We have a serious matter to discuss, but before we do, there are some pictures I'd like you to see."

There's a computer sitting on a table near the podium. Mr. Fetterly walks over to it and presses a button. Someone dims the gym lights. On the wall a photo appears of a vaguely familiar-looking guy with his arm in a sling. Using a remote controller, Mr. Fetterly advances the presentation to the next photo, which is of a house with a smashed-in front window, and then the close-up of a girl's face covered in lacerations and bruising. The most pathetic part of this photo is that the girl has tried to hide some of the damage by applying gobs of makeup, but it only creates the appearance of a gruesome Halloween mask. Next we see a guy lying in a hospital bed with a leg suspended in traction. He's hamming it up for the photographer: his tongue is lolling out of the side of his mouth and he's cross-eyed. A murmur of laughter ripples through the gym.

The next photo sobers the gym full of students again. This time it's of a car wreck, and it's clear that the vehicle involved is totaled. If the driver survived this crash, it would have been a miracle. Apparently it was.

The lights come back up and Mr. Fetterly shuts off the computer. "I'm sure you realize that the common denominator in all those photos was the game you call Gotcha. Those are the results of just a few of the incidents that have happened in past years, ones that I thought to capture on film.

"I have also brought a guest speaker to Slippery Rock to speak to you today."

We watch as Mr. Fetterly walks over to the door. He pushes it open, and we see a guy in an electric wheelchair roll himself into the gym. There is a woman with him, who remains standing by the door. The guy's face is pale and he has dark smudges under his eyes, but other than that he's every bit as gorgeous as Warren, and he appears to be about our age. Mr. Fetterly directs him over to the podium, where he's handed a mike.

"My name is Stephen Stewart," he says in a shaky voice. He glances shyly at Mr. Fetterly, who nods, encouraging him to carry on. "I live in Twin Falls, a couple of hours away by car. I graduated from high school last June." Stephen clears his throat. "Your principal asked me to come here today to talk about why I'm in a wheelchair." He sits quietly for a moment, staring at his hands, and then he looks up. "Some of the grads in my school played a game called Bang Bang

You're Dead, which is a lot like your Gotcha game, but we shoot our victims with water guns."

There's a murmur of voices and I suddenly remember the story that was all over the news a year ago.

"I was doing really well," he says softly, "and I was one of the final dozen survivors. It was getting hard because everyone was being so cautious.

"One night I decided to hide under my victim's car while he was at soccer practice. I thought it would be easy enough to roll out just as he was getting into his car, and I could get him."

There's a long pause. The gym is completely still. Stephen nods slightly. He raises the mike to his mouth, then drops it into his lap again. We can see him inhale deeply as he composes himself. Finally he clears his throat and continues. "It didn't work out as planned. The car ran over me before I could get out."

We wait, in pained silence. I wonder if he's finished, but eventually he carries on. "I'll never walk again, but I'm lucky to be alive." He doesn't look like he feels lucky at all.

I remember being horrified when I read Stephen's story in the newspaper, but seeing him in person, and hearing him speak…I have to blink back tears.

Mr. Fetterly takes the mike from him. "Thank you, Stephen, for coming to Slippery Rock today and sharing your story. You are a brave young man, and I hope your story will help our students realize the potential danger in the game that they're playing. With any luck, you'll have convinced them that it's time to stop once and for all."

Stephen just nods, turns and steers his wheelchair back toward the woman at the door, probably his mother. We sit in numb silence. I wonder if we should be applauding, but what would our applause be for? The fact that he survived? The woman holds the door open for him and he wheels away. As soon as he's gone, the quiet in the gym is disturbed by murmuring as grads discuss the incident. Joel, seated beside me, squeezes my hand.

"I brought Stephen here today, and showed you the photos," Mr. Fetterly says, "to remind you why the administration at Slippery Rock decided to ban the game of Gotcha this year. We had hoped that the strong leaders in your grade would enforce our decision, but as you know, that did not happen."

That hurts. I recall hearing this same slam on the class leaders from Mr. Bell.

"There have been complaints from parents about this year's game. To my knowledge, nothing too serious has happened, with the exception of some hurt feelings, but I feel compelled to ensure that nothing does happen. For that reason, I've decided to suspend from school any student who continues to play the game. As well, students who break this rule will not be allowed to attend grad ceremonies, not the valedictory ceremony or the dinner dance."

The quiet is again disturbed by muttering among the students. The sentiment is clear: Suspension is one thing, but taking away grad?

"Everyone's money is to be returned to them," Mr. Fetterly announces over the noise, "and the game is officially over."

Uh-oh.

Over the noise, a voice hollers out. "I thought you said we were here to discuss a serious matter." Tyson has risen to his feet and is confronting Mr. Fetterly. The gym goes quiet again. "I haven't yet heard any discussion."

"I guess 'discuss' was the wrong choice of words, Tyson, but I have made my decision, and I intend to stick by it. I'm sorry if you're unhappy with that decision."

"Unhappy is an understatement," Tyson says. "And besides, I don't know how you can suspend someone for doing something that has nothing to do with school. The game isn't a school activity. We're not playing it on school property. So what gives you the right to interfere with it?"

We all stare at Tyson, shocked at his disrespect, and then our heads swing back to Mr. Fetterly, who is managing to maintain his composure.

"Student safety is my business, Tyson. You've seen the pictures. You know what's happened. That's what gives me the right."

I see a note being passed down the row of students toward Joel and me. When it reaches me, I'm surprised to see my name on the front. I open it and read the signature first. It's from Warren. Glancing back down the row, I see him at the far end. We make eye contact, and he nods. I read the note. *Emergency grad council meeting, right after school, in the computer lab.* I look back at Warren and return the nod. He smiles and winks. I feel Joel glance at me. I just shrug and shake my head. No point trying to explain the weirdness between Warren and me. And it's only going to get weirder now.

Tyson is still arguing with Mr. Fetterly. He clearly has a lot invested in seeing the game continue. "Gotcha is just a game," he says. "We're not using water guns like at that other school. We're just using beads. There are a lot of things we could be doing that are way more dangerous."

"Tyson, the decision has been made." I can see the veins bulging on Mr. Fetterly's neck. "The game is over. Period. You are all dismissed."

The buzz around me is angry. Despite the guest speaker, even those who are no longer in the game are mad. Everyone wants to see Gotcha carried on.

"Are you okay, Katie?" Joel asks. He's handing me my crutches and is waiting to help me down the bleachers.

"Oh yeah, just ticked," I say. Though the truth is, my stomach has seized up. Stephen's story has really disturbed me, and what happens when people start demanding their money back? "And I have to meet with grad council," I tell him. "That should be fun," I say, thinking of Paige. I roll my eyes. "Not."

I give up on the crutches as I struggle down the bleachers. Joel offers me his arm, and I lean on him and put some weight on my foot. I notice it's starting to get easier.

"Do you want me to go with you?" he asks.

"Thanks, but I have to deal with it. She's bound to get over herself at some point."

Joel walks with me to the computer lab. "How are you getting home?" he asks.

"I don't know. The only thing I can think of is to stay at school until my mom gets off work and can pick me up."

"If I help you, do you think you could walk home?"

"Yeah, maybe." I have noticed a huge difference in my mobility today. "That would be great, thanks."

"Don't thank me," he says. "I just needed someone to link with."

I smack his arm and smile. How did I ever live without him?

Grad council is assembled and waiting for me. Paige has her arms crossed and is slumped in her chair. Warren grins when I enter the room.

"I hear a couple of council members are still scrapping."

I just shake my head.

"And you're still in the game, Katie?" he asks. "I didn't think that was your plan."

"Whatever," I say. If he only knew.

He gives me his famous smile. I wonder how dazzling it will be when I tag him. "So," he says, "we have to decide how to proceed."

"This sucks," Paige says. "We're almost there."

"I suggest we play it out," Warren says. "There's less than thirty people left, and Fetterly doesn't have to know anything."

There are nods around the room.

"But what about the people who want their money back?" I ask.

"I don't think that anyone who signed on to this game will expect us to quit at this point," Warren says. "We were banned from playing it in the first place, but look how many showed up, more than any other year We can't stop now. We'll just spread the word, quietly."

I realize how much my attitude has changed in the past couple of days. A week ago I would have jumped at the chance to cancel the game, especially after listening to Stephen's sad story. Now I desperately want to see it through. I want to see Joel get Paige's bead. I want to look in Warren's eyes as I tag him. But mostly, I don't want anyone demanding their money back.

"I agree, Warren," I tell him. "We've got to see it through."

Paige gives me a sharp look. "I'm surprised to hear *you* saying that. As I recall, I had to convince you to play it in the first place."

I can only shrug. "I've changed my mind."

"You sure have," Paige says, looking puzzled.

"Hands up if you think Gotcha should continue," Warren says. "Excellent!" he continues, glancing around the group. "It's unanimous. The game goes on, only no one is to speak of it."

"Maybe we should divide up the names of all the people in grade twelve and phone everyone," Michelle suggests.

"That won't be necessary," Warren says, studying me. I feel my face burn and I look away, but not before I see him smile at my discomfort. He knows the effect he has on me, and it makes me crazy. But that's all going to change. "I think the word will spread all on its own."

"I think you're right," Phillip agrees. "The word will be out before we'd get through half a dozen names. The joy of instant messaging."

Paige nods. "Okay, then that's it for the meeting?"

"That's it," Warren says. "Meeting adjourned."

As I struggle with my backpack and crutches, Warren says, "So tell us, Katie, are you and Joel official?"

"I don't know what official is," I lie, my face still burning, "but we've become good friends."

Warren nods. "I hope he makes you happy." He's smiling at me, but not his aren't-I-beautiful smile. This one looks thoughtful.

"So far so good," I tell him. I glance at Paige but she's picking at a fingernail. "See you guys around, then," I say, leaving the room.

"Yes you will," Warren says.

I find that with Joel carrying my pack, I can place a fair amount of weight on my foot, so the walk home isn't as difficult as I'd expected. I invite Joel in to check out the cookie situation, and the first thing I do is check my e-mail. There's still nothing from Dad.

"So, I was thinking," I tell Joel, after he's had a chance to eat half a dozen cookies, "that if I could find out from 'Riah what Paige is doing tonight, maybe we could flush her out."

"I think we should go after Warren's bead first," he says.

"Why?"

He takes another cookie. "I'm still smarting from being accused of using you to get to Paige."

"Well it's true, I'm still not sure about you…"

Joel sighs. "I'm trying to gain your trust, Katie, I really am. Can I help myself to some milk?"

"Right. I see where your priorities lie. Food first. Katie second."

"A guy has to keep his strength up." He grins.

I watch as he gets the jug of milk out of the fridge and pours himself a glass. "Whatever, Joel. I think it will be easier to get Paige's. I've always believed in getting the easy tasks out of the way first. Besides, she deserves to be tagged now."

"Okay, what's your plan?"

I limp back to the computer and check the screen. Mariah is online, so I know she's home. I pick up the phone and call her.

"Hey, Katie!" she says. "I hear the game's still on after all."

"You didn't hear it from me," I tell her.

"I didn't?"

"Nope. I want to go to grad."

"Oh, right. I get it. I heard it from someone else."

"So did I."

I can picture her on the other end of the line, her jet-black eyes shining.

"It looks like things are going well with Joel," she says.

I glance at him and feel myself blush. "Yep, pretty well."

Now he glances at me, noticing the change in my voice. I turn my back to him.

"So the reason I'm calling," I say, "is to ask you if you know what Paige is up to later tonight."

There's a hesitation, and I know Mariah is onto me. "Why do you want to know?" she asks.

I feel a twinge of guilt, knowing I'm asking Mariah to do something that will cause her friend to lose her bead, but I remind myself that we all signed on for this. "'Cause I want to try apologizing again," I tell her, amazing myself with my own quick thinking. "She probably told you that she wouldn't accept my apology, but I've got to try again. This whole feud thing is getting to me."

Mariah is quiet for a moment. "I expect Paige will be at home tonight," she tells me. "Like every night. She hasn't been going anywhere. Gotcha's really gotten to her."

"Okay, then maybe I'll drop by her house, see if she'll talk to me."

"Good luck," Mariah says in a tone that tells me she doesn't expect me to be successful.

"Thanks."

I hang up the phone and smile at Joel. "I think I just figured it out."

Joel picks me up at eight o'clock, and we drive over to Paige's house. He stays in the car, and I hobble up the walkway.

Paige's mom answers the door. She looks troubled to see me.

"Paige doesn't want me to let anyone in," she tells me.

"I know, it's the Gotcha game. But I really need to talk to her." The guilt is back. I'm coercing her mom into letting me do something that is going to make Paige go ballistic. *She signed on for this*, I remind myself.

"I don't know, Katie," she says. "I'm sorry."

"You've got to let me talk to her," I plead. "Maybe I can calm her down."

"Do you think you could?" she asks. I can see her weakening. She's clearly had enough of living with Paige in her paranoid state.

"I'm almost sure," I tell her. And it's true. She won't be paranoid when she no longer has her bead.

"Well, come in then," she says, unhappily, and backs out of the doorway. "She's in her room."

I leave my crutches at the door, lean on the banister to climb the stairs and limp my way down the hallway. I've been here countless times for sleepovers and birthday parties. This hall is almost as familiar as my own.

Paige's door is shut but I don't knock. I just open it and go right in. She's on the bed, lying on her side, a book propped up in front of her. She jumps, startled, and then glares at me. "What are *you* doing here?"

"I need to talk to you."

"We're finished talking."

"You might be. I'm not."

She climbs off her bed and goes to the door. "Mom!" she shouts down the hall. "I told you…"

I push the door shut. "Listen, Paige. I want to regain your trust." It hits me that I'm echoing Joel's words, but I decide to ignore that thought.

"I told you, it's over." I notice she won't make eye contact with me.

"Please, Paige, give me a chance."

"Forget it, Katie. We're through, so get out of my room!" She stands by the doorway, holding it open for me.

"I can prove that I'm a loyal friend."

She looks unimpressed. "How?"

"I can help you tag your victim."

Her eyes widen. "How can you do that?"

"Joel's hanging out with Elijah tonight. We're on our way to pick him up. You could be hiding in the backseat, and when he gets in the car…voila! His bead is all yours!"

Paige studies my face, looking suspicious.

"It's as easy as that, Paige. He won't suspect a thing. I'll be hiding in the backseat too. He thinks it's just him and Joel going out together."

"Why are you doing this, Katie?"

"Because I want you back in my life."

The acting was easy until this point. Now the guilt and shame are rising to the surface. I wish we could just get on with it. No more words.

I feel Paige studying my face. I sit on the bed and examine the bruising on my ankle.

"So Joel is setting up his friend."

"He's doing it for me."

"That doesn't seem very nice."

"It's how Gotcha is played."

"Would you do that to a friend?"

Is she onto me? "I guess it depends on how badly I wanted to win the game."

"And how badly do you want to win?"

"What are you getting at, Paige?"

She sighs and sits down on the bed beside me. "I had a break at school, so some of us went over to the mall for coffee. I saw you and your dad at the bank."

"Yeah, and? We had some chores to do."

"My dad told me that your dad isn't living at home."

Why didn't it occur to me that Paige's dad would know what was going on and would tell his family? They've been buddies for years. It's because they were friends that Paige and I became friends. "What's that got to do with anything?"

"Dad told me his problem has gotten…out of hand."

"What problem?"

Paige blushes. "You know…"

"No, I don't know."

"C'mon, Katie, of course you do."

"I don't know what you're talking about, Paige. What *problem* does my dad have?"

Paige stares at me, trying to read my face. "His gambling problem."

I stare at Paige, amazed. "His gambling problem?"

I laugh. "What are you talking about?"

Paige looks at me, confused. "You know he gambles."

"No he doesn't, he's an investor. He trades, on the computer. Every morning. I've watched him." He does. But as I talk, I realize I have no idea what he does with his evenings, and I've never dared ask. I remember the late-night fights with Mom. "He's onto something good right now," I tell her.

She looks embarrassed. "Whatever."

"He is!" Suddenly I'm desperate to convince her. To convince myself. "Really! I even lent him some money…"

Paige looks sharply at me. I look away.

"How much did you lend him?" Paige asks, whispering.

"Just a little…."

"How much is a little?"

I shrug. "Just some. I don't have much."

Neither of us says anything for a moment.

"You might never see it again, Katie."

"You're wrong, Paige." I can't believe her. "This is my father you're talking about. You know him." The words are spewing out of my mouth. "He's the guy who took us bike riding when we were little. And swimming in the pools at the river. You called him Yogi Bear and he called you Boo Boo. He's not a gambler."

Paige doesn't say anything.

I get to my feet, furious now.

"I can't believe you're saying this stuff, Paige. I know you're mad at me, but you don't have to spread rumors about my dad!"

"He borrowed money from my dad too," Paige says quietly. "He's borrowed it before, but this time is different. He seems to have disappeared. My dad doesn't think he'll see his money again. He wanted to trust your dad, he kept giving him chances, but now he figures your dad has a gambling addiction."

"He's wrong! It just takes time."

"The money came from *my* education fund." Paige is picking at her fingernails.

I look at Paige's face, and the truth dawns on me. In her twisted mind, she's blaming me for whatever she thinks my dad has done with money that was earmarked for her. That's why she dumped me.

"I've been e-mailing with him. I saw him. You said you saw me with him. He hasn't disappeared."

"How much money did you give him, Katie?"

I don't answer, but I can feel my face flush.

"You never wanted to play Gotcha originally," she says slowly, as if solving a puzzle. "But now you do. How come?"

I get up and hobble to the door. I don't need this.

"Katie, where's the Gotcha money?" she asks.

"None of your business."

"Katie, you didn't!" Paige springs to her feet.

I can only stare at her.

And then Joel is standing at the door. I'm numb. I can't move. My brain wants to tell him to leave, to go back to the car. But I can only stare at him. He looks at me, eyebrows raised, and steps into the room. Paige stares at him too, as if in disbelief. Then he reaches out and tags her. "Gotcha!" he says.

Eleven

aige stares at Joel. Then she turns to me. "You set me up," she says.

I say nothing. I still can't find my voice.

"I can't believe you'd do that." Her voice is a snarl.

Joel comes to my defense. "Paige, you told Katie that you were no longer friends," he says. "Until then, she made it clear she wouldn't help me."

Paige turns to Joel. "And who let you in the house?" she demands.

He smiles down on her. "The door was unlocked. I came looking for Katie."

"You can't just barge in!"

"No? Well I did. And I remember you just barging into Elijah's house not so long ago."

She glares at him.

He turns to me. "You were gone a long time." He tilts his head. "Are you okay?" he asks gently.

Before I can answer, Paige steps up to him. The top of her head barely reaches his chin, but she shoves him in the chest with both hands anyway. Then she turns to me.

"I hate you! You just wait. I'll get you back." Her face is flushed, and I notice her hands are shaking. "Get out of my house right now!" she says to both of us.

"I need your bead," Joel tells her. "And confirmation that your victim is Elijah."

"You know damn well it is!" she says, grabbing the bead that hangs around her neck and yanking on it. The silver chain snaps and she chucks the whole thing at him.

He reaches down and picks it up off the floor. He pulls the bead off and carefully places the chain on her desk. "You know how to take all the fun out of a game, Paige," he says quietly. "That's twice now." He reaches for my hand and leads me out of her room.

As I'm hobbling down the stairs, she's yelling, "I won't forgive you for this! You'll pay!"

Her mom appears at the front door just as we're leaving. "What happened?" she asks.

"Paige lost her bead," Joel says.

"Oh." She thinks about that and sighs. "Thank goodness."

I gather up my crutches and follow Joel to the car. Once we're in and the doors are locked, he turns to me. "What happened in there?"

I don't know what to tell him. Certainly not the truth. "She was just flipping out. You know how she gets."

"Uh-huh," he says, sounding unconvinced.

"And I'm not feeling well," I tell him, which is the truth. Now that I'm out of her house, I'm feeling even more nauseous. "Could you take me home?"

"But the fun is just starting, Katie! I need you to come and help me lure Elijah out."

"I'm sorry, Joel. I have to go home."

He picks up my hand. "Are you okay, Katie?"

I pull my hand away. "Yes, I'm okay. But I want to go home. Now."

I can feel Joel studying me. "Okay, no problem." I detect a hint of annoyance in his voice, but I can't help myself. I have to be alone. I really am feeling sick.

Joel pulls the car out onto the street and we drive along in silence. I'm trying to absorb what Paige has said about my dad. I think about the Gotcha money. I hope I don't throw up.

When we get to my house, Joel carries my crutches to the front door while I hobble on my sore ankle. I quickly thank him and go inside, ignoring his puzzled face.

I hear his tires spin on the loose gravel when he drives away.

Mom's watching TV in the living room. "Home so soon?" she asks.

I take the remote control off the coffee table and hit the power switch.

"What are you doing?" she asks as the TV goes off.

"We need to talk," I tell her.

"About what?" she asks, squirming uneasily in the armchair.

"About Dad."

She sighs and sits up. "What do you want to know?"

"Why did he leave?"

"We weren't getting along."

"Why?"

"That's between your father and me," she says.

"And me," I tell her. "I have a right to know. I'm still part of this family, in case you forgot."

"What happened tonight?" she asks. "Why the sudden interest in your dad?"

"Sudden interest?" I could spit at her. "I haven't known how to talk to you about him! You were acting like nothing was out of the ordinary around here."

Mom rubs her face with both hands. "To be honest, honey, it's been a relief to have your dad gone. He can't get at my money anymore, and I don't have to worry about what he's doing or where he is. Out of sight, out of mind, so to speak."

"He hasn't been out of my mind. I miss him."

"I'm sorry, Katie."

We sit in awkward silence for a moment. Then she gets up, shuffles to the kitchen and plugs the kettle in. She's wearing her housecoat and ratty slippers. It has always irritated me that she does nothing outside of going to work. She doesn't take classes, she has no hobbies or friends, and she doesn't exercise. She watches TV and makes cookies all weekend. No wonder Dad had to go out at night. This is all her fault.

"You didn't tell me what happened to prompt this conversation," she says.

I decide to lay it on her. "I was at Paige's tonight, and she said Dad has a gambling addiction."

Mom slumps against the wall between the kitchen and the living room. She crosses her arms across her ample chest. Her eyes shine too brightly as she studies the ceiling.

"Well, does he?" I challenge.

"I could never bring myself to say those words." She wipes her nose on the sleeve of her housecoat and shrugs. "I guess I've been in denial." She nods. "But Paige is right. I used to think of it as just a problem, but I suppose it's spiraled into a full-blown addiction."

"You're serious?"

Mom nods but doesn't look at me.

I collapse back on the couch. "How come I never knew anything about this?"

"I guess you chose not to see it."

"I chose not to see it? What are you talking about? You hid it from me!"

"For a long time your dad has been your hero, Katie, and for some reason I've been the bad parent in your eyes. You didn't see his faults."

The kettle whistles and Mom pours the water into the teapot. She sets it on a tray with mugs, brings them into the living room and settles herself back in the armchair. "I never knew what I did to make you dislike me so much, Katie. Maybe it was jealousy. You wanted your dad all to yourself."

"That's stupid."

She shrugs. "Anyway, your dad will never admit he has a problem."

I watch Mom pour the tea. "I don't believe this."

Mom doesn't say anything.

"How can you be addicted to gambling?"

"I'm not really sure because I don't gamble. But from what I know, once a person becomes addicted—to anything—they no longer have a choice. It's like a brain disease. I guess your dad has to gamble to make himself feel normal. Otherwise, he feels crazy."

"He said he was a day trader, whatever that is."

"I guess he was, though not very successfully. And maybe that's just another kind of gambling."

I kick the coffee table with my good foot. The cups rattle. "I feel so stupid! Paige knew and I didn't."

She nods sympathetically. "Paige's father has been a loyal friend to your dad. He's tried to help him, but I gather he's finally given up."

"Maybe you shouldn't have been so hard on him."

"Hard on him?"

"Yeah! You were always nagging him. Picking on him. Maybe you drove him to gambling."

Mom frowns. "I know it's hard to hear these things about your dad, Katie. But blaming me isn't going to solve anything."

"Maybe not," I tell her, getting off the couch. "But it might explain a few things!"

I storm out of the room and up the stairs to my bedroom.

Later, when I hear Mom shut the door to her bedroom, I go back downstairs and turn on the computer. I check for messages from Dad. Nothing. I check to see if Joel is on the chat line. He's not.

I pour myself a glass of milk and sink into a kitchen chair. I'm feeling a twinge of guilt about the things I said to Mom. But how could she say those things about my dad, her own husband? She and Paige are wrong about him. They have to be. He's invested the Gotcha money in something good. I know it. Won't they be surprised when they find out how much money I've made.

Maybe my last e-mail never got to him. That happens. I decide to send him another one and test him.

From: kittiekat17@hotmail.com
To: dannyo56@hotmail.com
Subject: $$$

hi dad so whats happenin with the investment? it looks like i'm gonna need the $ sooner than later. fetterly is makin us quit playing gotcha & im sposed to return everyones $$$. how soon b 4 i can get mine back?

my ankle is starting 2 get better. i can put some weight on it now. i hope everything is ok w/ u. pls write 2 me soon!

luv, katie

I wrestle with my blankets all night. Mom is wrong. I know my dad better than anyone. He's the soft-spoken guy who used to help me turn the living room into a campground on rainy days. We'd build a fire in the fireplace and nestle in our blanket-and-broomstick tent playing board games, giggling, making jigsaw puzzles and reading together with flashlights. We didn't even bother getting dressed or brushing our teeth. I smile, remembering.

But then I remember how these afternoons ended. Mom would come home and fume when she saw the mess we'd created, our breakfast and lunch dishes still lying on the kitchen counter, or on the coffee table, which was our picnic bench. I dreaded the sound of her car in the driveway because that meant the fun was over.

Dad is not a gambling addict. He just got tired of living with a cranky wife.

I alternate between doing homework and playing games on the computer all day Saturday, and I check for e-mails about every ten minutes. I try hard not to think about how quickly Dad got back to me when I told him I had some money, or how fast he showed up at the door.

Sunday arrives and I become even more fixated on the computer. Mom passes behind me and says ever-so-helpful things like "A watched kettle never boils." Dad memories are flooding my consciousness. I slip into their bedroom and open the closet. His clothes still hang there and I pull a shirt to my face, inhaling the lingering scent of his aftershave. I yank the shirt off the hanger and crouch in the closet, pressing it to my face. I can hear his tenor voice belting out love songs, and I imagine him downstairs, flipping pancakes in the kitchen. Then I hear my own squeals, and I squirm, remembering his whisker rubs against my cheek. He'd plunk me on the bath-room counter, and I watched while he applied shaving cream and then used the razor to scrape off the white foam. When the job was done, he rubbed his smooth face against my cheek.

I use his shirt to dry my eyes and wipe my nose.

Dad hasn't given me a whisker rub in years. We gave those up with piggyback rides and games of I Spy. Now that I think of it, as I went from being a little girl to a teen-ager, Dad went through his own changes. The whiskers didn't get shaved so often, and instead of hanging out or playing games with him, I'd have to tiptoe around him as he lay dozing in his housecoat on the couch each afternoon. I haven't heard him sing a love song in years.

Late Sunday afternoon, as I sit staring at a screen showing an empty in-box, I finally allow the truth to sink in. Dad is not going to write to me, and he's not writing to me because the money is gone.

Pieces of the puzzle that I'd never dared examine before start to slide together. The late nights. The fighting. I'm beginning to see a complete picture.

I run a bath and sit in the tub, allowing the tears to fall. My dad was my rock, the solid foundation of my life. I could always count on him. Now that the rock has crumbled, what can I believe in? Who can I count on? Dad loved me above all else. Why did he do this to me?

Neither Mom nor I speak during dinner. Mom slices her roast beef and shoves huge portions into her mouth. I try not to notice, but the noise of her chewing is making me sick.

By the time we're finished, I'm mad. Furious. My dad used me. Me! His only daughter. He knew I trusted him completely and he took advantage of that. And then he left me here. With her.

I'm also desperate. I've lost the Gotcha money. Now I have to win the stupid game. There's no other way out of this mess. I cannot tell my entire class that I gave away the money. Look what they did to me at Tyson's party. I can only imagine what this would set off. The photo Fetterly showed us of the girl with the lacerated face haunts me, and so does the image of Stephen in his wheelchair.

Back at the computer, I check the Facebook group page but it's gone. Odd.

Taking a deep breath, I dial Joel's number. He answers after a couple of rings.

"Hey, Joel."

"Katie." His voice is flat.

"Did you get your bead?"

"I did. And Conner's too. I'm up to four."

"Hey, way to go. And all on your own."

"Yeah."

"Who's your next victim?"

There's a long pause. "Guess."

Oh no. I put the phone to my other ear. "Me?"

He laughs. "No. But I guess we better talk about what we do if that happens."

"Yeah." Phew. He's beginning to sound more like his old self. "Who then?"

"Tyson."

"Are you serious?"

"Uh-huh."

"Oh my God."

"I know. And he's got lots of beads, so this is going to be so sweet."

Something tells me it's not going to be sweet at all, but I keep my thoughts to myself.

"So what happened to the Facebook group page?" I ask.

"Warren decided it had to go. If Fetterly found out about it, we'd all get nailed."

"Good plan." Once again I'm surprised by Warren's thinking.

"But I hear there are only twenty of us left."

"Huh." I might actually have a chance at this.

The line goes quiet.

"So," I say, feeling shy all of a sudden. "Are you still going to help me get Warren's bead?"

"You're feeling better?"

"Oh, yeah, sorry about that. Girl stuff, you know." Paige once told me that you can get a lot of mileage from that excuse.

"Oh. Why didn't you just say so?"

Paige also said that the boy would just say "oh" and drop it. She was wrong. "I don't know."

"That doesn't explain why you pushed me away, Katie."

"I said I was sorry. I really am."

He sighs. "You have a way of shutting me out, Katie. It makes me feel lousy."

"And I feel lousy about what I did."

There's a pause, and then he says, "Okay, you're forgiven this time, but don't do it again."

"I won't." I really hope I can keep that promise.

"Do you have any ideas about how to get Warren's bead?" he asks.

"I do," I lie. I'm just so glad he's changed the subject. "Can you come over for a while?"

"I can. I'll see you in fifteen minutes."

I check my reflection in the mirror and plant myself at the door, waiting for him to arrive. Mom is watching me from the kitchen. "You look like you're expecting someone," she says.

"I am." I haven't been able to make eye contact with her since Friday night. She hasn't spoken of our conversation, and neither have I. She's clearly more forgiving than I'd be, I'll give her that.

Joel arrives and we go into the living room. We're there less than thirty seconds when Mom appears in the doorway with a plate of cookies. I roll my eyes but Joel gives her his most charming smile. I'm beginning to think he shares some of the same attributes as Warren.

"Thank you so much, Miriam," he gushes.

"You're most welcome," she says, smiling. I get the feeling she thinks he's here to see her.

Joel takes a second cookie. "Would you consider giving me the recipe for these?" he asks.

"Of course," she says. "Do you like to bake?"

He looks embarrassed. "I usually just use that frozen cookie dough stuff," he says, "and the problem with that is I'm tempted to eat it frozen. Well, not just tempted. I do. In spoonfuls. And then there's no dough left when I want to make cookies."

She makes a face. "I'll write it out for you," she says. Joel laughs at her reaction and she finally leaves.

"So?" he asks, his eyes smiling at me. "What are those bead-snatching plans you referred to?"

I think fast. "Well, as you can see, I'm getting around on my foot a lot better than just a few days ago."

"Yeah, you are." He reaches for a cookie and takes two.

"But Warren doesn't know that. He still thinks I'm totally crippled."

"Right." He shoves a whole cookie into his mouth.

"So maybe I could phone him up and ask him to take me somewhere, or bring me something."

Joel studies me as if he doesn't quite get what he sees. "You think he's going to fall for that?"

"He's not the brightest light, you know that."

"Maybe not, but he's totally aware of who is still in this game and who isn't. I don't think he's going to get sucked into that trick."

"You're probably right." I know that, but I had to come up with something, seeing as I told him I'd thought it through. "Have you got any ideas?"

Joel shrugs. "Unfortunately, Katie, we've reached that stage in the game where we have to take extreme measures."

"Such as?"

"Well...for example, you could find a way of getting into his house and be there waiting for him when he comes home."

"You mean, like, breaking and entering?"

"Not necessarily. There are other ways." He thinks for a moment. "He has a little sister. Bribery might work."

"And if it doesn't? She'll tell him we bribed her and then he'll know one of us has him."

"Then we'll have to kill her."

"Joel!"

He throws his head back and laughs. "You should have seen your face, Katie."

I chuck a cushion at him.

"We'll just have to make the bribe worth it. She'd let us in for, say, one hundred dollars, don't you think?"

I feel my face burn. "I don't have one hundred dollars."

"You could borrow it from the Gotcha funds."

Our eyes meet. There's a question in his. I have to look away, scared that he'll see the truth in mine. What gave him that idea? "I couldn't do that," I say, feeling my face burn hotter than ever. "It wouldn't be right."

"I was just kidding!" He gives my shoulder a shove. "Lighten up, Katie." He watches me, clearly puzzled, but then says, "I could lend you the money."

"I'm not really into borrowing money. Too much risk."

"Fair enough." He nods thoughtfully.

"Any other ideas on how we could get into his house?"

"Maybe there's a key hidden outside."

"Yeah, and even if we find it," I say, "with my luck we'd set off an alarm when we opened the door."

"Okay, then maybe there's a doggie door you could crawl through."

"Joel!"

"Well, c'mon, Katie," he says, laughing, "let's hear your great ideas."

"I can lurk in the bushes, and when he comes out of the house in the morning..."

"Katie, that's been done. I'm sure he's been watching for lurkers. And you wouldn't be able to outrun him."

"Okay, then I'll find out where he's going to be after school one day. I'll be there too. And I'll stumble and fall, and he'll come help me up." I know how pathetic I sound.

Joel just shakes his head. "Katie, Katie," he says. "I told you. At this point in the game, no one with a bead will be found anywhere around town if they're not linked to someone else still in the game. And there are fewer and fewer people to link with. You're not going to find Warren on his own until this game is over."

I sigh. "Then I don't know. Can we follow him in your mom's car until he does something stupid?"

"I guess we could, especially if it were at night. But, like I said, I doubt he'll go anywhere alone."

"Is he still driving that pickup truck?" I ask. "The dark green one?"

"I think so."

I look out the window. It has grown dark. "Maybe he'll think he's safe under the cover of night. Maybe he's driving around right now."

"Maybe."

"Shall we go see?"

"Sure. At least we'd be doing something." Joel reaches for my hand and pulls me off the couch. "Let's go."

Mom isn't happy about us heading out so late on a Sunday night, but Joel assures her that we just need a coffee to wash down all the cookies we've eaten. She offers to make us coffee, of course, but when Joel tells her he's craving a nonfat, double-espresso, sugar-free vanilla latte, her eyebrows arch and she agrees that he'll have to go out for it. As the front door closes behind us, I swat his back.

"You're bad!" I tell him.

"I am not!"

"You've never ordered a nonfat, sugar-free anything in your entire life!"

"You haven't known me my entire life!"

"Just about!"

He grins and opens the passenger door for me.

As we turn onto Warren's street a few minutes later, Joel shuts off the headlights and we slowly creep down the quiet road, eventually pulling up to the curb across from Warren's house. He shuts off the motor. It feels surreal, this stalking, and suddenly I get the giggles.

"What?" Joel asks, smiling at me.

"I don't know," I answer and begin to laugh even harder. "This is just so crazy. Driving around without headlights. Spying on his house." Now I'm out of control. "Nonfat milk. Double espresso." I have to wipe away the tears that are running down my face. "We have to kill her!"

Joel starts to laugh too.

"Crawling in the doggie door!"

"Shhh," he says, between his own bouts of laughter. "He'll hear you from the house."

But I can't hold it in. Weeks of anxiety have found their release. Tears are streaming down my cheeks, and I cross my legs to keep from peeing myself.

Joel wraps one arm around my shoulder and clamps his other hand over my mouth. That works. The heat of his body is sobering. I look into his face and find him looking intently back, his breath warm on my cheek. I have to close my eyes and inhale deeply.

"Just nerves I guess," I say, peeling his hand off my mouth and exhaling at the same time. I reach into my pocket and find some tissue stuffed in it. I blow my nose and wipe my eyes.

We turn and look at the house. Warren's truck is parked in the driveway. There are lights on inside the house. "Now what?" I ask.

"We wait and hope he has to go somewhere tonight," Joel answers.

"Have you got a cell phone?"

"Yeah. Why?"

"You could phone him, disguise your voice, tell him you're a neighbor and you noticed that his headlights have been left on."

Joel nods, thinking about that. "I could."

"But?"

"But I don't think he's that stupid."

"It could happen."

"It could. But he'd send someone else out to check for him."

"So we could be waiting here forever."

"We'll give him an hour. Just long enough for me to drink that nonfat vanilla latte."

I smile up at him, and he leans forward and kisses me softly. His lips brush across mine. I shiver. "Are you cold?" he whispers.

I don't know whether it's his lips on mine or the cool night air that causes the shiver, but I nod anyway. He pulls me into a warm embrace. His cheek rests against mine and I can feel his heart pounding right through to my chest. We rock together, ever so slightly. I'm breathing in the smell of him and feeling so safe in his arms. I pull my cheek back across his skin, and my lips seek out his again in the dark. We kiss some more, and Joel twists his fingers in my hair. I forget about Gotcha, about gambling addictions, about money problems. Gone are worries about grad and my missing father. All that matters are Joel's lips on mine, and his hands that are now massaging my back through my jacket. I run my hands over his shoulders and down his arms. He breathes deeply, and his lips press a little harder into mine. Without breaking our kiss, his hands have moved around to the front of my jacket and he slides the zipper down. A moment later I feel the heat of his hands on my back, but now there's only the thin cotton of my T-shirt between his hands and my skin. I'm swirling further and further away from my worries, allowing my lips to respond to his, which are searching, searching...

Ping.

We jump apart, startled. Something has hit the roof of the car.

Ping. It happens again. At the exact same moment we turn and look across the street. Warren is standing on his lawn, grinning. He tosses yet another pebble toward Joel's car and we hear it bounce off the roof. *Ping.*

Twelve

We glance at each other. "Shit" is all I can think of to say, and I say it under my breath.

Joel rolls down his window.

"Busted!" Warren hollers across the street, laughing.

Neither Joel nor I say anything. We're too stunned.

"Couldn't you two find somewhere more private to make out?" he asks, grinning.

Again, neither of us answers. I can't make eye contact with Warren, and even without looking at him, I know Joel's face is as red as mine.

Warren tosses yet another pebble at the car. "I just happened to glance out the window, looking for stalkers, and voila! There you two are, just sitting here, casing my house. What a lovely sight."

Joel turns the key in the ignition and the engine fires up.

"Where are you going?" Warren asks. "Isn't one of you at least going to try to tag me? How am I going to know which one of you has my name?"

Joel presses the automatic switch and the window begins to close.

"Don't go!" Warren yells. Joel pauses with the window still half open. "I was enjoying the peep show," Warren says. "There was the kiss, the prerequisite hug…I was looking forward to seeing who would make the next move. I was pretty sure it was going to be Joel, but then Kittiekat looked like she was getting hot…"

"Shut up, Warren," Joel says and finishes winding up the window. He turns on the headlights and we pull away from the curb. I hear one last ping on the car as we head down the street, driving in silence. When we arrive at my house, Joel pulls up to the curb and shuts the engine off. I reach for the door handle, but Joel grabs my arm. "You're not pushing me away this time, Katie."

"I don't intend to," I say, though I realize I was just about to.

"Just ignore the stupid stuff he said."

I nod.

"He knows it's one of us, but he still doesn't know which one. And that's good."

I just nod. Being startled has left me feeling drugged, unable to think clearly, like when the alarm shocks me out of a deep sleep.

"Let it go," Joel says gently, pulling me closer.

I glance at my house, wondering if my mom is spying through the curtains on us. "Joel, can you let me out at the end of the block?"

"Sure." He looks at me, puzzled, but turns the key in the ignition. We pass about eight houses and then I tell him it's okay to park again. He turns off the car and pulls me back into his arms without a word. I gently push him away. He frowns. I lock the car doors and lean over toward him. His eyes smile at me, and then his lips are back on mine. I forget all about Warren.

Joel gets his mom to drop him off at my house Monday morning, and we walk to school together, arms linked. I've left the crutches at home, and I put a lot of weight on Joel's arm as I limp along beside him.

I attend my first class, turn in the project Mariah and I did together, and begin the long walk down the corridor to my next one. The halls are crowded, and I'm getting jostled. It makes me nervous that I could get bumped, forcing me to put all my weight on my sprained ankle. Maybe I've given up the crutches too soon. Eventually I make it to my second class, English Literature. I'm just settling myself into a desk when the phone, which connects each classroom to the office, jangles. Ms. Pearson picks it up, speaks into it and turns to look at me. She nods and then hangs up the phone. "Katie, Mr. Fetterly wants to see you in the office. Immediately."

My heart bangs in my chest. What could he want?

I leave my books on my desk and limp toward the door. "You better take your books with you," she says, not making eye contact with me.

I pause, puzzled, and go back to my desk to get them. The halls are empty now, and it's not far to the office. I walk as slowly as I can. I know something is wrong, but I haven't any idea what it is, and I'm in no hurry to find out. It could be a message from home, an emergency, but I doubt it. It must have something to do with the Gotcha game. But Fetterly doesn't know we're still playing, does he? Did someone squeal? Maybe he wants to know why I haven't returned all the money. I feel a bead of sweat trickle down one armpit, and I force my feet to move even more slowly.

Eventually I reach the office, and the secretary is clearly expecting me. She looks sympathetic but motions for me to go directly into Fetterly's office. He's sitting behind his desk, typing on a keyboard. He looks up when I enter and motions for me to take the chair opposite his desk.

"Katie," he says.

"That's right." I have no idea what I am supposed to say.

He wheels his chair away from the computer and turns to regard me. He's frowning. "Katie, I had a visit from Paige this morning."

"Oh." It takes a moment to register, but when it does, my stomach instantly clenches.

"She came to me to report that you are still playing Gotcha, even though I have banned the game and spelled out the repercussions to your entire class."

I can only stare at him. Why would Paige do this? She's going to have to answer to the entire class.

"You know what those repercussions are, don't you?"

I nod.

Fetterly taps his fingers on the desk. He sighs. "Paige, however, would only name you and refused to divulge the names of any other grads who are still playing," he says.

I continue to stare at him, uncomprehending.

He stares back at me. When he sees he's not going to get a response, he continues. "Katie, I've taken a look at your school records. You are one of Slippery Rock's finest students. You are on grad council. You've never been in trouble. Your teachers and classmates respect you. I know your name has come up as a possible recipient for many of our local scholarships. Potentially, a promising future awaits you. A suspension at this point in your life will seriously compromise all that."

His words hardly register. All I can think is *How could she do this to me?*

"Why did you continue to play the game?"

I look down at my hands. I know she was mad. I know she hates me for setting her up, but to go to Fetterly...

I hear Mr. Fetterly sigh and lean back in his chair. "Katie, as you know, I always follow through on what I say I'm going to do. I have to. It's the only way to run a school. Therefore, I'm going to have to suspend you."

I stare at my feet. I can feel my ankle throbbing.

"Unless," he continues, "you're willing to cooperate with me."

I look up, and our eyes meet.

"I would be willing to relax your punishment if you would name all the others who are still playing the bead game."

"Relax my punishment?" It's like I can hear the words, but they don't register in my brain.

"Yes. I would give you a two-day-only suspension and allow you to attend graduation ceremonies."

I regard him, still uncomprehending. "Allow me to attend graduation?" I ask.

"Yes, you don't want to miss that, do you?"

Now I realize that he, too, is uncomprehending. I finally find my voice. "If I ratted out the people who are still playing Gotcha," I tell him, "there would be no way I could attend graduation."

He tilts his head, puzzled.

"They would kill me."

"I think you're exaggerating, Katie."

"You're right. They wouldn't kill me. They would torture me slowly, painfully, and for the rest of my life I would be known as the person who snitched on the Gotcha players."

"You're getting carried away…"

My mind takes me back to that phone conversation I had with Warren after Tyson's party. What was it he said? *You know what happens when you anger the Gotcha Gods.*

He's right. The Gotcha Gods will haunt me for the rest of my life.

"The Gotcha Gods?" Mr. Fetterly asks.

Did I say that out loud?

"C'mon, Katie. I think this game is beginning to get to you."

I look directly into his eyes. "You're right, Mr. Fetterly, it is. I will take my suspension and miss grad. There is no possible way I can give you the information you're looking for."

Mr. Fetterly looks sad. "You go home and think about it, Katie. If you change your mind, come and talk to me." He pushes a piece of paper across his desk. "Now that I know the game is still being played, I'll find out who the other players are anyway. It might just save us both a lot of trouble if you'd write their names down now, before you leave."

I shake my head.

"They'll never know how I found out."

"Oh yes they will," I tell him. "It's those Gotcha Gods…"

Mr. Fetterly regards me closely. "Would you like me to make an appointment for you to talk with someone?" he asks gently. "Like the counselor? It doesn't matter that you're under suspension." I can feel him staring at me.

"No thank you."

There's a pause, and then he's all businesslike again. "Okay then, I'll be phoning your parents this afternoon," he tells me. "You're free to leave. Please don't come back to the school until such time as you are invited to do so, or until you're willing to talk to me again." He wheels his chair back to the computer and, shaking his head, resumes his typing.

I limp out of his office and past the school secretary. I go straight to the front door and hobble across the schoolyard and down the street. Once again I have the feeling that I'm just an actress in a bad made-for-TV movie and if I were to look back, I'd see Paige standing at a window watching me leave, her arms crossed, a smirk on her face.

I don't worry about being tagged on my way home. Everyone is still in school. When I arrive home, I reach into my jacket pocket to get my key. I put it into the slot, but when I turn it, I notice the door isn't locked. That's odd. I know for sure that I locked it when I left this morning. I glance at the driveway and then down the street. Mom's car is nowhere to be seen.

I turn the knob slowly and push the door open. Right away I can see that someone has been in the house—or is still there. Looking down the hall toward the living room, I notice closet doors hanging wide open. The cushions on the couch have been pulled off and tossed onto the floor. My rational brain tells me I should get the hell out of here, but I also sense that the pieces of the puzzle don't fit. The door was unlocked. It was not a forced entry. We own nothing valuable, nothing worth stealing. Why would someone be tearing our house apart?

Very quietly I step into the kitchen. Drawers have been pulled open and are left hanging on their hinges. Food has been pulled out of cupboards and dropped on the counters or the floor. How strange is that? Why would someone go through the kitchen cabinets? What would they hope to find here?

And then I hear footsteps in the hallway above my head. They're clomping down the hall toward the stairs. I stand frozen where I am. There's no way I can get out of the kitchen before the intruder makes it downstairs. The person is making no attempt to walk quietly. I listen to each footstep on the stairs. Fifteen steps in all, and then they reach the main floor. They turn the corner to the kitchen. I swear my heart stops in my chest.

"Katie!"

"Dad?"

It takes me a moment to recognize him. He is days unshaven, and his hair hangs in matted strands. I can smell his body odor from across the room. His eyes are wide, startled to see me here.

"Why aren't you in school, Kittiekat?" he asks.

"I've been suspended."

"You have?"

I nod. "What brings you home?" I look around at the mess. He does too.

"I was looking for something I left here."

"What was that?"

"Oh, just something," he says vaguely. "Nothing important."

"Are you looking for money, Dad?"

His eyes light up. "Have you got some, Kittiekat?"

I shake my head and sink into a kitchen chair. "I gave it all to you, Dad."

He looks confused. He closes his eyes and shakes his head a little.

"You haven't answered my e-mails," I tell him.

"No, I'm sorry. The librarians have discouraged me from going into the library. That's where I went to use the computers, and to work."

"Work?"

"Uh-huh. Do my trading."

"Maybe if you go have a shower and a shave and pick out some clean clothes from your closet, they'll let you back in." I can't believe he's gone downhill so fast. Was I so blind that I missed all the clues that he was heading this way? Wasn't it just a few days ago that he was telling me he considered himself a lucky guy and that he was going to make me proud of him?

He looks down at himself, as if he didn't realize the state of his personal hygiene. Then he shakes his head. "Did you say you had some money I could borrow, Kittiekat?"

"No," I tell him, trying to keep my voice steady. "I told you that I gave you all my money, which really wasn't my money to give, which you knew. You told me you were going to invest it and triple my investment. I believed you, Dad."

He's staring at me, bewildered. It just makes me madder.

"I didn't know you gambled, Dad. I would never have lent it to you if I knew that."

His chin drops and he studies his feet.

"And now I've been suspended from school because of that stupid Gotcha game. Any day now I'm going to have to tell my entire grade that I lost all the money they trusted me with. I won't tell them I gave it to you, Dad, to lose. That would be way too embarrassing. I'll tell them I used it as a deposit to save my space at some college next year. Of course, I won't be going to college next year, or any year, because I've been suspended from school indefinitely, so I won't be able to graduate. And I may not even be alive after the Gotcha Gods find out what I've done.

"The Gotcha Gods?" he asks quietly.

Our eyes meet. His are just vacant pools, as if his soul has been sucked clean away. That makes his and mine both. A flood of tears overwhelms me, and I drop my head onto my arms. A long time later I feel a light touch on my shoulder, but I don't look up. I hear him leave through the front door.

The morning drags on. I don't leave the kitchen chair. Hopelessness is a paralyzing drug.

Eventually I move to the living room and flake out on the couch. I flick on the TV, and the talk-show host's face appears on the screen. It's like I'm sliding faster and faster down that waterslide, each day closer to the time when I'll make my own nightmarish appearance on his show. *You really didn't see the inherent problems with investing the Gotcha money with your gambling addict father, Katie? C'mon. Everyone else knew he had a problem.* I flick the TV off.

At noon the telephone rings. I don't answer it. Who could I possibly want to talk to? But it starts ringing again a few minutes later. I pick it up and slam it back down. It starts to ring again.

"What!"

"Katie, it's me, Mariah."

"Oh. Hi." Just hearing her voice brings a lump to my throat.

"I know what Paige did, Katie. It's horrible."

I can't respond. The lump has strangled my vocal chords.

"Everyone's talking about it. They're all furious with her."

I swallow, hard. "She only ratted out me, 'Riah. No one else."

"I know. She told me."

"How did it get this bad between us?" My voice is cracking but I don't care.

"It's the game, Katie. It's cursed."

I can only sigh.

"Joel and I are coming over after school," she tells me.

"What for? There's nothing you can do."

"We have to think of something."

"This is not your problem."

"You just hang tight. We'll be there soon."

I hang up the phone.

After cleaning up the mess that my dad created, I go back to sitting at the kitchen table, just watching the traffic go by. Eventually I see Joel and Mariah coming down the road together. I let them in and Joel crushes me in a huge hug. My eyes fill yet again, but I soak up his strength. When he lets me go, Mariah does the same thing. I feel an infusion of their energy, a sense of connection, and I begin to let go of the despair. Their presence alone brings me relief.

"Joel, you took a chance, being outside and not linked."

"You're worth it," he tells me, smiling warmly.

I shake my head at his foolishness, but I feel a warm glow on the inside.

"We have a plan," Mariah says, pulling open the door to our fridge.

"You do?" I ask, surprised. Joel plunks onto a kitchen chair and pulls me into his lap, wrapping his arms around me. I feel more energized by the moment.

Mariah pulls out a block of cheese and begins slicing. "We've decided that Paige's actions have changed everything."

I nod. "They sure have for me."

"The sense we're getting," Mariah says, pointing the cheese knife at Joel and then back to herself, "is that Paige is about to self-destruct."

"Self-destruct?"

"Yeah. She immediately realized her error in ratting on you. She may have achieved what she wanted—getting you suspended—but it backfired. In the cafeteria at lunchtime, Tyson began chanting, 'Paige squealed, Paige squealed, Paige squealed.' After a few minutes, someone else began to say 'Oink Oink' after each of Tyson's 'Paige squealed.' Before you knew it, half the room was chanting 'Paige squealed,' and the other half of the room was replying with 'Oink Oink.'"

"Oh my God." Part of me is intrigued, glad that Paige is getting it back, but the other half of me is feeling queasy. Paige and I were friends for a long time. I know she'll be mortified, and I actually find myself feeling bad for her. "What did she do?" I ask.

"She just picked up her things and went out the door. Tanysha went with her. The chant got louder and louder as they walked away. They went out the front door, and we assume they went home."

"She'll never show her face at school again," I say quietly.

Mariah brings a plate of cheese and crackers to the table. "I know," she says. "It's pretty sad."

I move off Joel's lap and we eat the snack quietly.

"So what is your idea?" I finally ask them.

"Well," Joel says, looking at me thoughtfully. "The most important thing is to get you back to school, right?"

"I don't know," I tell him. "Is that the most important thing? Or is it to win Gotcha?"

"You still intend to play?" he asks.

I shrug. "I haven't figured anything out. I'm still trying to figure out what the hell happened."

"What exactly did Fetterly tell you?"

"He said that if I ratted out everyone else who is still in the game, he'd shorten my suspension to two days, and I could go to grad."

Mariah's eyes widen. "But you said no?"

"There are some things worse than not going to grad," I tell her. "Though I am worried about what will happen to my whole year if I can't write exams."

I see the look that passes between Mariah and Joel.

"What?" I ask them.

"We were thinking…" Mariah says.

"You were thinking what?"

"That you can't rat everyone else out."

"Duh. I figured that out for myself."

"But you also can't stay suspended because of Gotcha."

"Right. So where does that leave me?"

Mariah glances at Joel and then back at me, "You have to take the Gotcha money to Fetterly and tell him you can't rat everyone out, but you are turning it over to him to do with as he pleases. Maybe he could create a Gotcha scholarship or something. But that would make the game officially over, you haven't squealed on anyone, and the money could be used for something worthwhile. I think everyone would find that more acceptable than any of your other options."

I look first at Mariah, then at Joel. "You guys are nuts."

"You don't think it will work?" Mariah asks.

"I know it won't work," I tell her—because there is no money, but I can't tell them that. "What would Tyson and Warren do to me if I turned it all over?"

"They'd be a whole lot madder if you turned them in," Joel says. "And right now that is what they're worrying about. They know a person like you is not going to throw away her entire year of school for the Gotcha game."

"Thank you, both of you," I tell them. "I'll think about it, but I don't know…"

"What choices do you have?" Mariah asks.

I can only shrug. That momentary feeling of connection with my friends is fast fleeting.

"Katie," Joel says, "there is not an easy solution. But this might be the best compromise."

"Yeah, tell Tyson and Warren that."

"I know," Joel says. "They won't be happy. But at least they're not suspended."

"And in a way, they both save face. Neither of them has to lose the game," Mariah adds.

"That's true," Joel says. "I didn't think of that."

I hear my mom's car pull into the driveway. I look at the clock and see that she's early. "Uh-oh," I tell them. "I think Mom's heard from Fetterly. You guys better leave."

"Will you think about what we said?" Mariah asks.

"Yes," I lie. I hear the car door slam. "Go out the back door," I say. "Quickly. I don't know what she's going to be like."

Joel takes my face in his hands, kisses me and follows Mariah out through the back door of the house just as Mom comes in the front.

Thirteen

Mom's face is pale and she's puffing as she stomps into the kitchen. When she spots me at the table, she stops dead in her tracks. "What the hell is going on?" she demands.

I can only shrug. "I got suspended."

"So I heard," she says, eyes bugging. As she stares at me, I see the color returning to her cheeks, but she begins to breathe harder. "Well? Are you not going to explain?"

"I'm sure Fetterly already did."

"I'd like to hear your side of the story." She drops her purse on the kitchen counter, pulls out the chair across from me and plunks herself in it.

"I got caught playing Gotcha so I got suspended. End of story."

"I told you that game was bad news, Katie. Why didn't you listen to me?"

I shrug again. There's no way to explain the pressure to her. She just wouldn't get it.

Mom stares at me until she realizes she's not going to get an answer. Then she says, "Fetterly said he gave you an option, that you could return to school immediately if you so wished."

"Did he tell you what that option was?"

"No. He said that was between you and him."

Grudgingly, I offer up a silent thank-you to Fetterly. "It was an impossible option, Mom. Believe me, if I took it, my life would be in serious danger."

"You've got to be kidding."

"I'm not."

"We're talking a stupid game here, Katie, not organized crime."

"It amounts to much the same thing."

She just stares at me, totally exasperated.

"Think of the bright side, Mom," I tell her. "I no longer need money for a grad dress. And you won't need to buy banquet tickets or photos or any of those other things you couldn't afford."

"Katie, think about what you're saying." She leans aggressively across the table. For the first time I notice gray streaks in her hair. "You have to get into that school right now and bring an end to this. You are a smart girl! You could have a wonderful future! I can't believe you'd get so caught up in this nonsense that you'd allow this to happen."

"Well I did, Mom. It's happened. There's a lot of stuff you don't understand, and there's nothing I can do about it."

"Help me understand it." She leans back and folds her arms across her chest.

"I can't. You just wouldn't."

"And you're just going to sit there and accept that."

"I don't know what else I can do."

I can't look at her, but I feel her glare. It's a standoff. I can hear her short puffs of breath. The windows rattle as a truck passes by. Eventually she breaks. "Well you better think of something!" She pushes her chair away and stomps across the kitchen, slamming shut a cupboard door. I hear the creak of the stairs and she heads to her bedroom.

The day can't get any worse. My life can't get any worse. A heaviness descends upon me, and I can't even muster the energy to leave the kitchen table. I lay my head down.

Some time later the phone rings, but I ignore it. After six rings the answering machine clicks in, but no one leaves a message. Then it begins to ring again. "Katie, get that!" Mom hollers down the stairs. As I limp across the kitchen to pick it up, I silently pray that it's Joel. He's the only person in the world I want to talk to right now.

"Katie."

It's not Joel. "Warren."

"I hear you have a little problem," he says.

I know he's panic-stricken, wondering if I'm going to turn him in, but his voice is as come-on and sensuous as ever.

"Not a little problem. A big one."

"I wish I could help you out."

"Sure you do."

"I do, Katie, I really do." He says it in a way that, if I didn't know him better, I'd believe him.

"I don't see how you can."

"Did Fetterly want to know who else was playing?"

Warren must really be nervous. I didn't expect him to come out with the real reason for his call quite so soon.

"Yes, he did."

"And did you tell him?"

"Not yet."

His sigh of relief is not audible, but I hear it anyway.

"Are you going to?"

"It depends on how badly I want my suspension to end."

This time I hear the sigh. "This is quite the predicament you're in, isn't it?" He doesn't need to spell out all the facts. We both know what they are. What surprises me is he sounds like he actually cares.

"It's even worse than you know, Warren."

"Really? How could it be worse?"

"It just is."

"Trouble with Lover Boy?"

"If you mean Joel, no. We're fine."

He hesitates. "Then what do you mean?"

It must be his voice. Or maybe it's that I've sunk to a place so low that I just don't care anymore. When I open my mouth I find myself telling Warren the truth. "I lost the money."

"The Gotcha money?"

"Yeah."

"How could you lose it?"

"I just did, okay?"

"Did you spend it?"

"No! I lent it to someone, someone who has… disappeared."

"Maybe they'll reappear."

"That's not likely."

For a moment Warren doesn't say anything. I even begin to wonder if he's hung up, but then I hear a little chuckle. The chuckle grows into a laugh and then builds into a hysterical, deranged-sounding noise. I have to pull the receiver away from my ear. "So we're all running around stalking each other for nothing?" he asks between fits of laughter.

"That's right."

"Oh my God! That's hilarious!" he hoots. "What were you going to tell the winner when you couldn't pay up?"

"I have to be the winner. There is no other way."

That shuts him up, and instantly I regret my confession. What creepy thing will he do with that information?

"Does Joel know about this?"

"No. I'm too embarrassed to tell anyone. I don't even know why I told you," I say in a whisper.

"Well, there's only one thing left for us to do then," he says.

"What's that?" I wait to hear the details of my torture.

"Make sure you win."

I can't have heard him correctly. "Are you serious? You're not going to kill me?"

"Jesus, Katie! It's just a frickin' game! Sure, it's been fun, but this is ridiculous. Enough is enough."

I'm not sure whether to believe him. "Not everyone is going to feel the way you do, Warren."

"I know." He sighs.

"And what about the Gotcha Gods?"

"Get a grip, Katie." He pauses, thinking. "The thing is, you need to tell Fetterly it's over, the sooner the better. Like tomorrow. Tell him we decided to quit."

"Huh?"

"Yes. The game has to end tonight."

"Easier said than done."

"I'll make it happen."

"Why are you doing this, Warren?"

"Because I want your body."

"Shut up."

There's a long pause. "I do. But that's only part of it." He laughs and then clears his throat. "Maybe because you didn't rat us out when you had the chance."

"I couldn't. Tyson would have killed me."

"You're right. His competitive gene is overdeveloped."

"So I still don't get it. Why would you help me?" I ask again.

There's another long pause. "Because, Katie, for the first time, you've treated me like someone."

"Like someone?"

"I know what you think of me, Katie. You think that I'm a male bimbo."

He's right. I feel my face burn.

"And maybe I am. We each do what works for us." He clears his throat.

I'm stunned. This is the first time I've ever heard him sound anything but cocky. "But I've always admired you, Katie. And just now, when you confided in me…" He pauses, clearing his throat again. "It felt like you might actually have some respect for me. Like maybe you do like me after all."

"Of course I like you."

"You've never acted like you do. You act like you think you're better than me."

I'm feeling so awkward. So ashamed. How did we go from the Gotcha game to this? The worst part is I suspect he's right. "I think I was just jealous because you beat me out for class president." I laugh, but it comes out like a silly nervous titter.

"I'd have handed the title over to you if I thought you'd take it," he says. "But I know you're too proud."

"You're right. And you won it honestly."

There's an awkward moment. "So how do I go about winning the game?" I ask finally.

"Do you have my name?" he asks.

I pause, alarmed. Have I just fallen for another Gotcha trick? Suddenly I don't care. "Yes," I confess. Now that I've told him about the money, I'm feeling a huge weight off my shoulders. Nothing has changed, but I don't feel so all alone.

"Perfect. I'll be able to hang onto my bead then, and you'll have yours. When we're the last two people in the game, I'll give you my bead and voila. It will all be over. No one will know."

He makes it sound so easy. I feel my hope returning.

"Whose name do you have?" I ask.

"Joel's."

"Oh no." All sense of hope disappears again.

"What's the matter?"

"We're working as a team."

"You *were* working as a team."

I shake my head. "He'll hate me if I don't stick with him. I can't do it."

"Don't be silly, Katie. Of course he won't hate you. Of anyone in our class, he'd be the first to understand. He strikes me as being totally level-headed. He won't mind at all if he knows it gets you out of this mess."

Could he be right? Oh God, I hope so. Things are just getting good with Joel. I don't want to mess with that.

"So that's where we have to start," Warren says. "And immediately. You invite Joel over and then let me in. It will be quick and painless."

Painless. I feel sick. I promised Joel, told him I was his partner. Would he do this to me? No. So how can I do it to him?

And yet...maybe Warren's right. Joel knows what's at stake for me. Well, he doesn't know about the money. What would he think of me if he knew about that? But he did tell me that he's just playing the game for fun, that he's not obsessed with it. Not like Paige was.

Paige. Oh man. I will have set up my two closest friends, Paige and Joel, before this is all over. What have I become? And did I betray my entire class by loaning Dad the money?

Just when I thought I was at the bottom of that water chute, I slide a little farther.

"Katie? You still there?" Warren asks.

"Yeah."

"So can you get Joel over? Right now?"

"Right now?"

"We've got to wrap this up tonight, remember?"

"Okay. I'll call him."

"Good. And unless I hear otherwise, I will be at your door in an hour. Just let me in and I'll tag him."

"He's going to be so mad."

"Katie. We have to do this. We have to get you back to school."

"Okay. I'll see you in an hour."

I hang up the phone and quickly dial Joel's number before I lose my nerve.

"Hello?" Joel answers after just one ring.

"Joel, it's me, Katie."

"Hey, Katie." His voice softens when he realizes that it's me. Now I feel sicker than ever.

"Something urgent has come up and I need you to come over right away."

"What is it?"

"I'll explain when you get here."

"But…"

"Can you come?"

He hesitates. "Not really but…" He sighs. "Yeah, okay, I'll be right there."

I flop onto the living room couch while I wait for Joel. I'm hoping my mom doesn't decide to appear from her room to serve brownies during the tagging. That's just what I'd need. I'm surprised she isn't in the kitchen cooking up a batch right now. That's her usual stress-buster.

The wait is killing me. I see some books lying on their side in the wall unit. Dad must have knocked them over when he was ransacking the house. I straighten them out, placing them back on the shelf in order of their height, tallest to shortest. Then I arrange the rest of the shelves the same way. I stand back and admire my handiwork.

I move from there to the kitchen, where I tackle the spice rack. I wipe off each bottle and replace them in alphabetical order.

Still no sign of Joel.

I start organizing the papers and CDs that collect around the computer. What could Joel be doing? He said he'd be right over.

Just when I'm about to start cleaning the elements on the stove, the doorbell rings. Thank God. Feeling ill at what I'm about to do, I hobble to the door and open it up, expecting to see Joel, but it's Warren who's standing there, peering past me into the house.

"You're early. He's not here yet."

He doesn't look at me but slides past and walks straight through to the living room. "That's okay," he says. "I'll be able to tag him as soon as he arrives."

I nod. "I did wonder how I was going to explain to him why I'd called him over."

As I follow him down the hall, an idea blindsides me. I could reach out, tag Warren and stay in the game with Joel. I could. Why don't I?

But then I remember. Warren knows my dirty little secret. What would he do with that information if I tagged him right now?

I sit across from him and study his face as he scans the room. I try not to think about what being indebted to him might mean.

The silence is awkward. Warren fiddles with his phone, opening and shutting it. His presence fills the room. I am so aware of him, yet I try hard to remain aloof. He turns suddenly and smiles at me, a warm, reassuring smile. I feel my skin burn and look away. Why do I get so messed up around him?

"We can do this, Kittiekat," he says softly.

I just nod, still not looking at him. He saved me once before, at Tyson's house. I just hope he can do it again.

I think about what he said, how he didn't think that I liked him. Was he serious? And even if I didn't like him, why would he care? Everyone else loves him.

I wonder how a person acquires that kind of magnetism. Do you learn it or are you born with it?

When the doorbell rings, my stomach clenches. I make eye contact with Warren, and he nods, ever so slightly. When I hesitate, he smiles again, that same smile that has opened so many doors for him. Disgusted with myself, I hobble down the hall and open yet another one.

Immediately Joel's arms are around me. I look up and he's grinning, all sweetness and innocence.

And then I know that I cannot go through with it.

I push him away. "Run!"

"Huh?" The smile turns to confusion, but he drops his arms.

"Run! Warren is going to tag you."

I give him another push. He steps back, but he doesn't leave.

That's when I hear the footsteps behind me and see the alarm on Joel's face. Now he does turn to run, but it's too late. Before Joel even gets out of the doorway, Warren smacks his arm.

"Gotcha!" he declares. Then he turns to me, his hand in the air for a high five. I ignore it.

"Katie?" Joel asks, looking back to me.

"I'm sorry, Joel," I say. I turn away so he can't see my tears.

"Did you set me up?"

I open my mouth, trying to find words to explain, but Warren interrupts. "She sure did," he says, putting himself between Joel and me.

"Why haven't you tagged *him*?" Joel asks, even as Warren is pushing him out the door."

I wanted to! The words are screaming in my head, but nothing comes out of my mouth. It would require such a long explanation.

"Give me your beads, Joel," Warren says. "And your victim."

"Katie," Joel calls, "was the whole thing a joke? Did we ever have a real alliance?"

I want to tell him the truth, tell him why I had to do it, but Warren is pulling him down the driveway, and Joel appears to be too stunned to put up a struggle. I move to the kitchen and watch from the window as Joel passes Warren his beads. Before he leaves, Joel glances back at the house one more time. When he sees me in the window, I mouth the words again. "I'm sorry."

He just stares back, and I watch as his bewilderment turns to something much harder. He gets into his mom's car and squeals away from the curb.

For the millionth time today, I lay my head on the table and wish I'd never heard of Gotcha.

Fourteen

I feel Warren's hand rubbing that hollow space between my shoulder blades. My initial reaction is to shrug it off, but even that requires too much effort. I give up.

"He'll get over it, Kittiekat," he murmurs. "He will."

"Whatever."

"And we're almost there."

I raise my head and look at him. "I forget why you're doing this, Warren. There's no money, remember?"

"I'm doing this to get you back in school."

"There must be an easier way." There must be. I just can't think of what it is right now.

"Listen. You stay put. I'm going to go nab a few more beads, but I'll be back as soon as I can."

I must be hearing things. "You're going to *nab* a few beads? If it was that easy the game would have ended by now."

"I have a plan."

"And what is that?"

"I'm not telling, but it's a good one."

"If it's such a good one, why haven't you already won this stupid game?"

"Shh, Katie." Warren puts his fingers to his lips and peers around the room.

"What?"

"The Gotcha Gods. You called the game 'stupid.'" He glances over his shoulder. "They might be listening."

I smack his arm. "Shut up, Warren!"

"We need all the help we can get right now."

I roll my eyes but make a silent apology to the Gotcha Gods. Warren's right.

There's a creak in the upstairs hallway. We both glance at the ceiling. I hear the bathroom door shut.

"When you come back, just tap lightly on the door." I glance back at the ceiling. "She goes to bed early."

"Better yet," he suggests, "text me."

"I don't have a cell phone."

"Oh. Right. Then just call my phone when she's gone to bed."

I get his number and see him out the door. Then I turn on the computer and check my e-mail. Nothing. Has Dad really dropped off the planet?

Mom comes down the stairs and plugs in the kettle. "Did you have any dinner?" she asks.

"Yes," I lie, not wanting to have a meal with her. "I made myself some eggs."

She roots around in the fridge and pulls out a container with leftover casserole. She sniffs it. "How old do you think this is?" she asks.

I think about it. "Too old," I say.

I watch as she scrapes it into the garbage and goes back to the fridge. There's a slice of apple pie that she brings out, and then she reaches for the ice cream in the freezer.

"That's your dinner?" I ask.

She gives me a look. "No comments from the school dropout."

"I'm not a dropout. I got kicked out."

"No you didn't. You have choices."

"And so do you," I say, glancing at the pie. "They're just not too appealing right now, are they?"

Mom gives me another look but doesn't respond. I admit, in some ways she has better self-control than I do. She knows when to bite her tongue.

The kettle whistles and shuts itself off. Mom pours herself a cup of tea and takes her "dinner" to the living room. A moment later I hear the drone of the TV.

The phone rings and I pick it up.

"Hello?"

"Katie?"

"Hey, 'Riah." Uh-oh.

"Katie! I heard what just happened. How could you do that to Joel?"

"I didn't want to, 'Riah, but I had to. Warren has a plan to get me back to school, and that was part of the plan."

"You trust *Warren*?"

"Yeah."

"Why?"

"Because he rescued me at Tyson's, and I think he can do it again."

"I wouldn't trust him."

"Hey, I didn't see you sticking up for me at the Gotcha party."

The connection appears to go dead. I wonder if she has hung up.

"Joel is super-upset," she says finally. "He came straight here after Warren tagged him."

"Is he still there?"

"No, but Katie, he was hurting, bad."

Oh man. "I feel terrible about it, 'Riah, but I had to do it. You've got to believe me."

"You've blown it with Joel."

My heart sinks even lower. "You don't understand."

"What don't I understand?"

"Just...something that happened."

"And what was that?" She sounds skeptical.

"I can't tell you."

"Why not?"

"'Cause you'd hate me."

"I wouldn't hate you!"

"You might when you hear what I did."

"Is it worse than what you did to Joel?"

"Yeah."

"But Warren knows?"

"Uh-huh."

"So you trust Warren more than you trust me?"

"It's not that. It's because he promised to help me out of my mess."

"So did Joel and I!" Mariah is getting steamed. "We don't make promises we can't keep, but we were trying to help as best we could."

"I know." I do.

"So what was it that you did?"

There's nothing else to do but tell her. "I lost the Gotcha money."

There's a long pause. "You lost it?"

"Uh-huh. I lent it to someone, and now I can't get it back."

"How could you do that? It wasn't your money!"

"I thought I'd get it back, plus a lot more."

"Katie," Mariah says very quietly, "this does not sound like something you would do."

"Well, I did."

"There's got to be more to it that you're not telling me."

I cannot bring myself to tell her who I gave the money to and why. It's so pathetic. How could a father do that to his daughter? "That's all I can tell you, Mariah. And Warren swears he can bring this game to an end tonight, with me being the winner so that I don't have to give anyone the money. And that's why I had to set up Joel."

"Why would Warren do that?"

"I don't really know. But he said he would."

"I still don't trust him. And I don't think you should either."

"I have to, 'Riah. It's my only hope."

I hear the click as she hangs up on me.

I have just swooshed out of the waterslide chute and crashed onto the jagged rocks. My friends, my dad, my self-respect, gone. I've been kicked out of school, and I won't graduate. And now I've put all my trust into an untrust-worthy person.

How did I get to this place?

Before Mom goes to bed, she drags herself back to the kitchen. I think she's planning to give me another lecture, but when she sees the shape I'm in—head resting on the table, face blotchy red and the floor littered with sodden tissue—she changes her mind.

"Sometimes things look better after a good night's sleep," she says.

I try to nod. "Thanks, Mom."

I hear the toilet flush in the upstairs bathroom, and when I hear her cross the hall to her bedroom, I call Warren's cell.

"She's in bed," I tell him when he answers.

"Good," he says. "I've got them, all but one."

"You do? How could you?" He's only been gone a couple of hours.

"I do."

"Come on over."

I let him in and we sit at the kitchen table, talking in hushed voices.

"You don't look so good, Kittiekat," Warren says, studying my face.

"I don't feel so good either." He runs a finger down my cheek, but I bat his hand away. "How did you get them all, and so fast?"

"Easy," he says, unperturbed by my rebuff. "First of all, we were down to eight players anyway."

I nod.

"And since the game went underground, there's been more confusion about who has whose name."

"Right."

"And do you remember who wrote out all the names on the scraps of paper?"

"Wasn't it Paige?"

"No, it was me."

"So, what does that have to do with anything?"

"When I left here, I went home and cut up some more scrap paper, exactly like the originals."

I can only stare at him.

"And I wrote the name of each of the remaining players on those pieces of paper."

"You're kidding."

"Nope."

"That's cheating!"

"Show me where in the rulebooks it says you can't do that."

"Warren!"

"So, one by one, I tagged the remaining players, except for one. None of them realized that I didn't really have their names. "

"I can't believe you'd do that."

"Really?" He regards me coolly. "And I can't believe you'd give the Gotcha money away."

I feel my face flush.

"I could have done it the legit way, just tagged them one at a time and kept taking their beads and their names, but this sped the process up because I could tag them in any order." He gave me a searching look. "And as you know, Kittiekat, we don't have much time."

"But they'll figure it out eventually, when they start talking."

"Probably, but I'll just feign innocence. Tell them I had each of their names, which I did."

"I think they'll kill you."

"Me? Warren MacDonald?" He laughs. "Not a chance."

Hmm. I wonder if even Warren has that much immunity.

"How did you get close enough to tag them? No one trusts anyone right now."

"Except me. Everyone trusts me."

Even me. I'm such a fool. "What exactly did you do?" I ask.

"I dropped in on each of them to discuss important school business."

"Important school business? They bought that?"

"Of course. You see, there was a strong possibility that you were going to blow the whistle on each of us and get us suspended, so we had to have a Gotcha Game Time-Out to discuss what we were going to do about the situation."

"A Gotcha Game Time-Out?"

"Yeah, clever, don't you think?"

"And each one of them fell for it."

"Each one of them did."

At first I don't believe him, but then I remember his seductiveness, that hypnotic voice and the acting skills. Maybe it really was that simple.

"And then you just tagged them."

"Just like that."

"Didn't they go crazy and accuse you of cheating?"

"No, I think they were too stunned by what had just happened." He grins. "Aren't I clever?"

I have to smile. I honestly can't believe the nerve of this guy.

"So who is the one person you didn't get?"

"Tyson. And Tyson has your name."

Just as I'd figured. "That one's not going to be so easy to get."

"Oh yes it is. I have a plan."

"Another one."

"Yes."

"And does this one require cheating too?"

"Oh no. We'll tag Tyson fair and square."

I sit back and listen while Warren fills me in.

Apparently Tyson was surprisingly calm when Warren phoned and told him that we were the final three, but that I was going to blow the whistle on them unless they handed me their beads. Tyson called me a bitch, but agreed, reluctantly, that it was better to give up the game than get suspended. He said he'd meet us at the park to do the exchange, but said he couldn't get there for another hour.

"Why the park?" I ask. There's something wrong with this picture.

"I'm not sure," he answers, frowning. "But then again, why not? Too many parents hovering about anywhere else."

"Phone him back. Tell him I'm not going to the park. We can take his beads right here in my driveway."

"Don't sweat it, Kittiekat. It's just Tyson's way of being a big shot. We'll be together, we'll stay linked, just in case, and it'll be no big deal."

"Forget it," I tell him. "I'm not going to the park. That's way too creepy. He must be up to something."

Warren sighs but punches Tyson's phone number into his cell phone. I hear him tell Tyson that I refuse to meet him in the park.

"Is the parking lot with the drive-through coffee place okay then?" Warren asks me. He's holding the phone to his chest.

I think about it. It's wide open. Not much could go wrong there, unlike the park, where anyone could be lurking in the trees, even the Gotcha Gods…I still think it's odd that Tyson won't just come here, but I've trusted Warren this far so I might as well go the full ride. I nod.

Warren and I wait in his truck, drinking coffee. I think back to the afternoon that Joel and I sat in this same parking lot. I thought things were bad for me then. I had no idea how much worse they had yet to get.

Warren keeps checking his watch, and his foot is twitching nervously.

"Is something wrong?" I ask him.

"What could go wrong?" he says, smiling brightly, but he can't mask his agitation.

"I didn't ask if anything was going to *go* wrong. I just wanted to know why you seem so tense."

"I'm good," he says, taking my hand and squeezing it. "We've got this nailed." Then he checks his cell phone to see what time it is. "He should be here any time now."

The minutes drag by, but eventually I hear the sound of Tyson's car squealing around the corner, the boom box blaring. He pulls into the parking stall one away from ours.

Warren and I climb out of his truck and face Tyson, who has also stepped out of his car, looking amazingly calm for a bloodthirsty guy who is about to lose his bead. Without any fanfare, Warren tags Tyson's arm. "Gotcha," he says.

"Oh gee," Tyson says sarcastically. He hands a long piece of hemp with beads over to Warren, winking as he does so. Warren shoves the beads deep into his pocket.

I look at Warren, confused. What was the wink for? In the very next second, Warren reaches over and tags me. "Gotcha!"

"Huh?"

Tyson laughs and high-fives Warren. "Hey! We got her good, man!" he hoots.

I look to Warren, stunned. "What?"

Warren is ignoring me, grinning. "No, man," he says to Tyson. "I got you *both* good!"

Now Tyson and I look at each other. He's as shocked as I am.

"You're screwing me?" Tyson's eyes are bulging out of their sockets.

Warren is doing a little victory dance in the empty parking stall between our two cars.

"Hey, man!" Tyson stammers. "We were a team!"

I see the red creeping up his neck as he watches Warren. I feel my own adrenaline surging. Tyson balls his hands into fists and shoves Warren against his car. "There's no messing with me, asshole!"

I shove past Tyson and slam both of my fists into Warren's chest before he regains his balance. "What the hell is the matter with you?" I scream into his face. "You know there's no money."

"No money?" Tyson asks, puzzled.

"There are other ways for you to repay me," Warren says, ignoring Tyson. Before I can stop him, he leans forward and presses moist lips onto mine.

My rage appears to give me superhuman strength, or maybe the Gotcha Gods are at work, but whatever it is, I shove him in the chest and, despite his size, he falls back against the car. "You've screwed practically everyone!" I yell again. "What is your friggin' point?"

"The point is," he says, unfazed and straightening his shoulders, "that this is a game, and I'm the ultimate winner. I outsmarted our entire class. No one will think of me as just a pretty face again."

"You won't *have* a pretty face again," Tyson says and reaches into the back of his car.

I glance in the rear window and see a baseball bat lying there. Part of me is alarmed, but the other part is excited. Warren can't be allowed to get away with this.

As Warren scrambles to get into his truck, I notice a long snake of vehicles pulling into the parking lot. They form a blockade around us and, one by one, members of our class emerge from the cars. Warren slams shut his truck door and presses the automatic door-lock button.

"What's happening here?" Liam asks, walking up to where Tyson and I are standing.

I happen to know that Liam is one of the unlucky people who lost their beads tonight.

"Katie and I were just letting Warren know how we feel about the way he plays Gotcha," Tyson says, cradling the bat and stroking it as if it were a soft animal.

Liam nods. He motions to the other people who are standing by their cars. "That's why we're here too. We've been chatting online and realize that the Pres messed with us all tonight."

Someone leans into their car and beeps the horn. This is answered by a spattering of other beeps.

"Thanks, Tyson, for letting us know that you were meeting Warren here tonight. We spread the word and decided to join you and give Warren what he needs—his own Gotcha Game Time-Out."

"Oh yeah," Tyson agrees. "That *is* what he needs. What are you thinking of?"

"We're thinking of the city park. We thought we'd take him there, force some apologies out of him, then leave him for a prolonged time-out."

"I like the way you think," Tyson says. "Do you want me to help you get him out of his car?"

"That would be great," Liam says with exaggerated politeness.

Tyson takes a swing at the back window of Warren's truck and it shatters. I jump back as glass falls in beads at my feet. Tyson reaches in and unlocks Warren's door, pulls it open, and he and Liam haul Warren out of the truck. More shattered glass falls to the pavement.

Warren puts up a struggle, but four more guys have come forward to help. He's shoved into the back of Tyson's car with a couple of bodyguards to keep him still. Tyson climbs into the driver's seat and starts it up.

For a moment I wonder if Tyson is going to question me about the money, but he seems to have forgotten all about it. Everyone is focused on Warren, so I'm off the hook for the time being.

I'm invited into another car, and the caravan pulls out of the parking lot and heads toward the park. For one creepy moment I feel like I'm part of a funeral procession, but then I remember what Warren has done to me, and his punishment cannot come soon enough.

Fifteen

The road leading into the park slices through the forest and is long, winding and dark. *Park Closed Between Dusk and Dawn* signs are posted at intervals, but there is nothing to physically stop us from entering.

When we reach the clearing, the cars are parked and everyone gathers around a smirking Warren, whose arms are being held by two bodyguards. Liam is also there, and he's carrying coils of rope. I see people taking swigs from various kinds of bottles. It's a clear night, and the light from the stars and moon illuminate everyone's faces.

"Off to the pond," Liam instructs and he leads the way along a narrow path. Flashlights are switched on and I hobble along behind, reveling in anticipation. Retaliation will be so sweet.

The park borders a river that is popular in the summer for its swimming hole and beach, but we're heading in the direction of the group picnic area, which features a duck pond in the center. When we reach the grass field, we gather around Liam again. He seems to have taken on the role of Warren's Time-Out warden.

Liam turns to Warren, who is still being restrained by two larger guys. "All your clothes off," he orders.

The group begins to cheer and egg Warren on. I hear myself cheering with them. Warren simply shrugs and starts with his jacket. Someone begins to hum the tune of a strip-tease song, and Warren pretends to get into it, grinding his hips and swinging his jacket over his head. We whistle and clap. Warren drags the dance out, and the hysteria mounts. I feel my heart pounding, excited by the noise, the cold air sharpening my senses. The traitor will pay.

When Warren gets down to his boxer shorts, he stops for a moment and scans the crowd. When he sees me, our eyes meet and are glued to each other for a moment. Then he grins and winks. After that the shorts are off and the crowd goes wild.

Something about that moment instigates my crash back to reality. Looking into his eyes, I see the raw fear. The wink is his cocky way of hiding it, but it is there.

I remove myself from the circle and slide into the shadows of the trees. It's like a plug was pulled on my adren-aline rush, and it's swirling down a drain. Something bad is going to happen, and someone needs to stop it. When the class ganged up on me at Tyson's party, Warren came to my rescue. Now it's my turn. I know I have to do something, but I feel paralyzed. I can't get my mind and body to work in sync to come up with a plan.

Liam, who is deftly twirling Tyson's baseball bat over his head, orders Warren to stretch out on the grass.

The goons force him down, and long lengths of rope are tied to each of his hands and feet. "So, Warren," Liam asks, "do you have anything to say to your classmates, the ones who you deceived tonight?"

"Yes," Warren says from his place on the ground. "Thank you!"

Wrong answer. A roar comes from the gathered crowd. Liam orders that Warren be pulled to his feet and marched over to the pond. Different people are assigned to hold the ropes. "In you go, Mr. President," Liam says, and four more guys lift Warren off the ground and throw him into the water.

Warren is dragged back and forth across the pond, thrashing. The crowd whistles and cheers. Bottles appear from hidden pockets.

Just when I think I'm going to throw up, Liam calls for Warren to be brought out of the pond. He is led away from the water and stands in the center of the circle, his arms wrapped around his body for warmth.

"So, Warren," Liam says. He appears taller than usual, enjoying his dictatorship. "Is there anything else you'd like to say to your classmates about your despicable behavior tonight?"

Warren stands tall and proud, still gorgeous despite his forced swim. "Yes," he nods. "I'd like to thank you all for being so gullible, making it so easy for me to steal your beads."

An empty beer can is tossed at Warren's head, and then another. "Back in the pond," Liam orders.

Warren is dragged through the mucky water for another five minutes. I'm still hidden in the trees, shivering. I think about walking away, but something keeps me here. If I leave now, how far will they go? Maybe I can talk some sense into them if it gets too crazy.

Once more, Warren is pulled out of the pond and asked to make an apology. He's shivering hard, but he's still standing tall. He scans the crowd, looking for someone. "Katie, wherever you are, thank you for putting your faith in me. You're the best!" I can see people glancing around, looking for me, but I'm well-hidden in the shadows.

Tyson steps in and takes over as Warren's Time-Out warden. "Back down on the ground, Warren."

When he doesn't move, the goons step in and force him down. Tyson then unzips his fly and pees on Warren's chest. There are screams of horror as well as cries of approval from the crowd. When Warren's dragged back up, Tyson zips up his fly and asks, "Anything you want to say now, Mr. President?"

Warren turns to Tyson and spits. The goons yank him back to the pond, the frenzied crowd egging them on. I'm too numb to move.

The next time Warren is pulled out, he still refuses to apologize, but he looks blue with cold.

"Let's warm him up!" someone says, and he's pushed to the ground again. This time he curls into a ball while the streams of urine spatter off his cold skin.

I drag my eyes away, repulsed, and that's when I seem to wake out of my stupor. My arms and legs become unstuck, and I creep over to where Warren's clothes lie in a heap and reach for his jacket. I check each pocket, looking for his cell phone. When I find it, I flip open the cover and punch in 9-1-1.

By the time the police arrive, the frenzied mob has bound Warren to a tree with the rope and is dancing around him, chanting "Time-Out, Time-Out." Someone has gagged him with a sock, and he's trembling, violently. I'm the first to spot the flashlight beams coming down the trail, and then a German shepherd bounds into the clearing. There's a surreal moment when everything appears to stand still, frozen. The grads gawk at the police, and the police stare in horror at Warren, tied to the tree. Tyson breaks the bizarre stillness first, dashing into the forest. Then everyone scatters, with three police officers and the dog in pursuit.

I help a female officer untie Warren. I bring him his clothes, and the officer asks him if she should call an ambulance. He shakes his head, but he's still trembling. He allows her to put her own jacket over his shoulders even though it's way too small. He doesn't make eye contact with me, and the cockiness has completely disappeared. Then the three of us make our own way back along the trail to the parking area.

When we reach the patrol car, we are both asked to sit in the backseat while the police officer starts the ignition and turns up the heat for Warren. His hands are pressed in his armpits and he's shaking miserably. I can see some of the others sitting in the back of another car, while still others huddle in a group, waiting for directions.

The officer speaks into her radio and then turns to look at us.

"Were you the one who made the 9-1-1 call?" she asks me.

"Yes."

"Why didn't you call sooner?"

I can only stare at my hands and shrug. I feel her studying me for a moment. Then she leaves the car, and I watch her approach the group standing in a cluster.

"It was the Gotcha Gods," Warren whispers. His arms are wrapped around his body, but the trembling is easing up.

"Huh?"

He turns and looks directly at me. "The Gotcha Gods. That's why you didn't call them sooner." He's dead serious.

I stare back at him and then nod. Yeah, I guess it was.

Warren reaches into the pocket of his jacket. He pulls out a handful of beads that are all tangled up together on a thin cord and drops them into my lap. Then he pulls out another handful, on a broken string, and then another. He heaps them onto my lap. I stare at the plastic beads, worthless objects, probably bought at a discount store, looking nothing like the glossy orbs that we'd each been given at the start of the game. They're just like the paper that money is printed on. Valueless, until we give them worth.

"What are you doing?" I ask.

"Take them," Warren says.

I turn and stare out the window. I see Tyson being escorted into the back of another patrol car. "I don't want them." I collect up the heap and dump it back onto his lap.

"But the money..." Warren says.

"You won. Remember?"

"But you rescued me. Even after...Just take them."

I scoot as far away from him on the seat as I can. He's still thinking about the game, even after what he's just been through. "It's over, Warren."

He studies me and then shoves them off his lap. They lie between us, a couple of hundred beady eyes, staring up.

Sixteen

I take a quick glance at the bleachers that are filling up with my classmates but go back to staring at a vent in the side wall. Years ago, at my grandpa's funeral, I discovered that if you stare intently and without blinking at a single object, it helps check the tears. I haven't figured out what to do with my trembling hands, though, or the nausea. I picture myself puking, right here, in front of everyone, and never being able to show my face in public again. Maybe I won't be able to anyway, after this humiliation is over.

I think back to Tuesday morning, when Fetterly came to see me. He'd been hearing various reports of the incident, and I ended up spilling my guts to him. Mom sat in shocked silence, staring at me as if I was a complete stranger. She'd only heard an abbreviated version the night before when I was delivered home by the police. After hearing my story, Fetterly shook his head and paced the living room. I could see his jaw muscles flexing as he clenched and unclenched his teeth. Then he sighed, deeply, and said, "I'm going to have to give everyone, all thirty-five of you, a week's suspension, as I said I would. Grad privileges will also be taken away."

"The valedictory ceremony too?" I asked.

He considered that. "No, you can attend that."

I nodded.

"But you, Katie, will return everyone's money, even if it's in installments."

I slouched farther down on the couch.

As he was going out the door, he turned back to me. "Do you understand how everything got so bad, Katie? Why it spiraled out of control?"

"No, not really."

"Then think about it. I'm calling another grade twelve assembly for tomorrow morning, and I want you to tell everyone there exactly what you've just told me. The rumors are buzzing around this community, and I want the story set straight by someone who was there. Perhaps you can even give us some insights on how it ever got to the point it did."

He started to leave again, but turned back once more. "And maybe your grad class can come up with a way to redeem yourselves. In a few weeks you'll be leaving Slippery Rock, and on a very sour note I'm afraid."

Now Fetterly taps on the mike, hushing the noisy gym. "As you all know," he says to the assembled crowd, "an... an incident occurred this past Monday night." The flexing jaw muscles are at it again. "As a result, thirty-five of your classmates have received one-week suspensions and will not be attending the grad dinner and dance. I dislike having to enforce this punishment, especially at this point in your year, but you were all told what would happen if you continued to play the game. And I believe that everyone who was at the park on Monday night was still involved. Not directly perhaps, but enough that they need to suffer the consequences." He waits while the sudden chatter dies down. "Katie is going to speak to you today and explain exactly what happened on Monday night so that we can bring a stop to the rumors." When he continues, he sounds completely exasperated. "I have fielded dozens of phone calls and e-mails from your parents, so I expect you to go home later today and tell them what Katie is about to tell you."

He hands me the mike and moves away from the podium. I walk behind it, needing something to lean on.

I hadn't realized the mike was so heavy. I raise it to my mouth with no idea of what I am about to say. Then I find my mouth has gone completely dry. There's a glass of water on the podium, but when I try to sip from it, I find my hands are shaking so hard that I can't hold it steady enough.

"You'll all remember," I say, testing out the mike and finding that it works, "that Gotcha was banned as a school activity this year."

The gym has become completely still. I'm tempted to look up, check to see that everyone is still there, but I decide to keep my eyes firmly glued to the glass of water.

"A lot of people felt ripped off, so the grad council decided to run the game outside of school. I wasn't crazy about the idea, but I went along with it because it seemed like the majority of people wanted that. I collected the money and put it in my bank account for safekeeping."

Deep breath.

"I guess things started off okay, but personally, I managed to trip and sprain my ankle the first weekend of Gotcha while trying to beat my mother to the front door in case... well, you know. Then there was that party at Tyson's, and for those of you who attended, you'll remember that there was an incident...not as serious as the one this past Monday, but serious enough in my mind. It was bizarre, and I decided to drop out of the game."

I pause for a moment, trying to remember what happened next in the chain of events. I glance up at the bleachers, and instantly my eyes connect with Joel's. The hurt in them is too much, and I return my gaze to the water glass. Sighing, I carry on. "In hindsight, I really should have followed through and quit right then and there. Instead, I figured out another way to get even with everyone."

The gym is still quiet. I continue. "My dad, who isn't living with us, e-mailed me and asked if I had any money to invest. He swore that he could triple my investment almost immediately."

I wonder, now, why I never questioned that. I also remember how quickly he was there to collect the money from me.

"So...I...I lent him the Gotcha money."

Now the gym comes alive. I can hear the outrage, but it gives me a chance to take some more deep breaths. I go back to staring at the vent.

Eventually the gym grows quiet again and I continue.

"As you know, Mr. Fetterly decided to stop the game. He said the money was to be returned. I thought that was going to be a problem for me, but fortunately," I pause, "well, maybe not so fortunately as it turns out, the game continued underground. But then I got caught playing, and I was suspended."

The murmuring increases again. "I did not want to turn everyone else in," I tell the crowd, "but I *did* want to graduate, obviously, and…" I sigh, "my dad had disappeared with the money."

The trembling in my hands has increased to the point where I can hardly hold the mike still. "You see," I say, clearing my throat, "what I didn't know until just recently was that…" I have to stop. The words won't come out. I look helplessly at Fetterly.

"Carry on, Katie," he encourages.

I swallow and stare hard at the glass. "What I didn't know was that…that my dad has a gambling addiction."

The gym erupts, but I hardly notice. I feel myself crumple inward, and I can't stop sobbing. I feel, rather than see, someone take the mike from my hand. It's Fetterly. He shuts off the switch and speaks to me quietly. "You're doing a great job, Katie. And this is very important. Take your time, and when you're ready, carry on."

When the sobbing finally stops, someone passes me some tissue. I mop up my face and find myself staring at the floor, trying to sort things out. My head is aching, but I know I need to finish. I suck in deep, ragged breaths, pick up the mike and switch it back on.

I speak over the noise. "Warren came to me then and I broke down and told him the whole truth. He seemed to think it was funny and assured me that he could help me win the game so that I wouldn't be expected to pay out any money to anyone else. He also led me to believe that I'd be able to return to school if the game was over."

I pause, thinking about that. Did I really believe it would be that simple?

"Warren proceeded to trick seven of the remaining eight people out of their beads," I say quietly. "Then we only had to capture Tyson's to win, and he had a plan to do that. What I didn't know was that Warren had also formed an alliance with Tyson. Tyson thought he and Warren had set me up, and they were going to win and could then split the money."

The crowd has become completely still again. I've reached the part of the story that they are probably most curious about.

"In the end, Warren had set us all up. He won, even though he knew there was no money. He said he just wanted to prove that he could do it, but when people started talking and realized how he'd won, they got angry."

I consider telling them that Warren and I call the source of that anger the Gotcha Gods but decide against it. I'm looking stupid enough right now.

I force myself to finish the story. "Warren was taken to the park, where he was stripped and dragged through the pond several times." I pause and close my eyes, not wanting to relive that night. "At first I got right into the spirit of it. I wanted retaliation too. But when people started…started peeing on him…" I shake my head. "I called the police, and they came and broke up the mobbing. Warren is going to be okay. Fortunately, it didn't get any worse than it did."

I could stop here. I've done what I was told to do, but I find myself still talking. "The weirdest thing about it, for me, is that I became one of the mob. Possessed. I never thought that could happen. It was like…me, the real me, got lost inside somewhere. And all for a stupid game."

Mr. Fetterly starts toward me, clearly thinking I'm done, but I shake my head and continue, even though my voice becomes increasingly shaky again. "I've learned a lot about myself, and it's not good stuff." My eyes are burning and I close them for a moment. Then I continue. "I was not a good leader for our grade, for you." I look over to Mr. Bell, who nods. Then I look back at the water glass. "I'm sorry I let you down. I also learned…I learned that I'm just like my dad. I gambled, and lost. I took advantage of my best friends the same way he took advantage of me. I didn't know how he could do that to me, and I don't know if I can ever forgive him." I find Joel's eyes again. "I don't expect my friends to be able to forgive me either, for the same reason." Joel looks away.

The gym is still.

"I promise to return your Gotcha money to each of you."

I shut off the mike and Fetterly takes it from me. "Thank you, Katie, for clearing it all up for us."

I walk away, toward the door, ready to start my week of suspension, but I hear him say, "Fortunately, we can learn from our mistakes. We don't have to make the same ones twice." I keep walking. "And the human species has a huge capacity for forgiveness. Class dismissed."

Seventeen

I can feel my ankle ache as I count the money I made in tips tonight. Another twenty dollars for the Gotcha fund. I've been back at work at the restaurant for three weeks, and I have enough money to repay exactly twelve Gotcha players. Only two hundred more players to go. At this rate, I'll be out of debt to them about the time I'm being hauled off to an old-age home. Oh well. Anything to appease the Gotcha Gods.

After tipping out and saying good night, I push through the doors into the warm spring night.

The headlights of a car in the lot blink on and I hear the engine start up. It's been five weeks since the Gotcha game ended, but I still feel my stomach knot up when I'm alone—which is most of the time. For a moment I envision Tyson in that car, with his goon friends, stalking me...but this time it's not my beads they're after...

I shake off the feeling and start walking home, but then I feel the car pull up alongside me. I take a closer look and recognize it as Joel's mom's car. The window rolls down. "Need a lift?" he asks.

I haven't spoken to Joel since the night Warren tagged him. We've all become masters of avoidance. Seeing him now, with a shy smile, I feel the walls caving inside me. I have missed him so much. I look past him into the car. Mariah is sitting in the passenger seat, and she's smiling shyly too. I haven't spoken with her for five weeks either.

I shrug. "Thanks," I say and slide into the backseat.

"We're thinking of getting a couple of nonfat, double-espresso, sugar-free vanilla lattes," Joel says, his eyes briefly meeting mine in the rearview mirror. "Are you in?"

I smile, appreciating the effort he's making to put me at ease. The last time he'd said he wanted one of those, it was only so my mom would let us out of the house. "Sure."

When we arrive at the coffeehouse, we order our drinks and sit in a booth, Joel and Mariah across from me. I study their faces, wondering what the reason is for this sudden friendliness, but their faces don't offer any clues. I take a sip of my latte and ask, "So how have you guys been?"

"Pretty good," Mariah nods, glancing at Joel.

"Yep," he agrees. "Can't complain."

"Got your grad dress?" I ask Mariah.

"Actually," Mariah says, "I'm not going to grad."

I'm stunned. "How come?"

"Well, to be honest, our hearts aren't really into it, with everything that's happened, you know."

"Are you serious, 'Riah? You were all about grad a few months ago."

"Yeah, but that was before. So many people can't go now, because of…of the incident, and, well, we thought we'd skip it too."

"You're not going either?" I ask Joel.

He just shakes his head.

I stare at them, amazed, and wonder what I would do, given a choice…"So what's happening with all those expensive dresses that won't be getting used now?"

Mariah just shakes her head. "There was an uproar about that," she says. "But you know Fetterly. He won't back down."

"We'll go to the valedictory ceremony," Joel says. "And wear the gowns and caps and hopefully get some scholarships and all that."

I nod. Scholarships. I'm back to earning a small wage, but all my tip money is being used to repay the Gotcha players, so my bank account is still looking pathetically empty. I'm beyond hopeful about scholarships. I'm counting on them.

"Thank God everyone's still allowed to go to that," Mariah adds.

As we sip our drinks I remember how anxious I was a few months ago about getting a nice grad dress. Now it's hard to believe I thought a stupid dress was so all-important.

Joel clears his throat and fiddles with a stir stick. Then he says, "Katie, I really…really admired how brave you were to tell your story at that assembly after the Warren incident, especially the personal stuff, about the money, and your dad…"

"Fetterly made me do that."

"I know, but still, you made us all realize that it takes just one bad choice and things can change," he snaps his fingers, "just like that."

Mariah nods.

"It made me think," he says, "that for us it was Gotcha, but for someone else it could be drugs or crime…"

"Or gambling," I add.

"Yeah," Joel says. "I won't judge people so quickly anymore."

We sit and think about that.

"So, if we've become so understanding," Mariah asks, "how come the spirit has been sucked out of our class?"

I look at her. "What do you mean?"

"Take us, for example. We don't want to go to grad."

"Why not?" I still don't really get that. Especially from Mariah, who loved the idea of dressing like a princess.

She hesitates and blushes. Then she studies the foam in the bottom of her cup. "So many friendships ruined because of that game. It just won't be the same."

The silence becomes incredibly awkward. I study the bottom of my cup too, but finally decide to ask the question that can't be ignored any longer. "Why did you guys pick me up tonight?"

Neither of them says anything for a moment. Then Mariah speaks. "We've decided we need to put the game behind us before the year is over and everyone has moved on." She looks directly at me. "We don't want to remember our grad year this way. It's our last chance to make things right."

"And how are we going to do that?"

"We're not sure," she says. "But we've got to start by talking about it."

So we sit for another minute, still not talking. I try to lighten the mood. "How about a healing circle, the kind the Tlingit people do?" I tease, recalling the project that the two of us worked on together.

Mariah smiles back at me. "Wouldn't that be hilarious? All two hundred plus of us in a circle, passing the talking stick and getting everything off our chests."

"What are you guys talking about?" Joel asks.

Mariah explains. "In the Tlingit culture, everyone who is affected by a crime is brought together and sits in a circle."

I'm impressed that she remembers this. It was covered in my part of the project.

"They have a stick," she continues, "and only the person holding the stick can talk. Each person gets a chance to speak, and you only get a second chance after everyone has had a turn."

"The point of it," I add, "is that the victim gets to tell the person who harmed them how it felt, and the person who did the harm gets to explain why they did it. In our system, everyone is protected from one another by lawyers. In the Tlingit way, more understanding and healing supposedly occurs."

Joel is nodding. "I can see that. When you have to look directly in the eyes of someone you've hurt, you start to really understand what you've done."

I look at Joel, not believing that he could ever hurt anyone.

"I think it's a great idea," he adds.

"What is?" Mariah asks.

"The healing circle."

"But there's way too many of us," Mariah says, laughing.

"But we could start right here, with just us."

Mariah and I study him, wondering if he's serious. His eyes have lost their twinkle, so apparently he is. Then Mariah looks at me, her head tipped.

"Could we wait until Paige and Tanysha can join us?" I ask, panicky. Clearly I'm the one who's going to get dumped on here.

"You can have another one with them," Joel says. "I think we should have our own, right now, while we're here together."

Mariah and I look at each other. Her eyebrows arch. "Well?" she asks me.

I shrug. "Okay." I must be nuts. "But we need a talking stick."

Joel grabs a knife lying on the table in the next booth. "Here it is."

"I said *stick*, Joel, not weapon."

"It will do," he says, clearly impatient to get on with this. "Who goes first?"

Mariah and I look at each other. "I don't remember that part," she says. "The person with the knife, I mean stick, I guess."

Joel nods, grasps the knife, point up, and rests his fists on the table. He thinks about what he's going to say and then clears his throat. He talks directly to the knife. "I'd like to tell Katie how it felt to be betrayed by her." He pauses, and I hold my breath, waiting for his words. "It totally sucked." I let my breath escape. "I thought things were going really well between us," he continues, "and me and Mariah would've done anything to help her out, but instead of trusting us, she turned to Warren, who was not her friend. She pushed me away again, after promising not to. I couldn't forgive her for that."

My face burns. Joel's right about how this works. I do totally get what I did and how he felt.

Mariah places her hand over Joel's and says gently, "Joel, I think you're supposed to speak directly to Katie, not to the talking stick."

He nods, briefly makes eye contact with me and passes the knife to Mariah. "I was finished anyway," he says.

I slump down in the booth, feeling terrible. I wish I could change what I did, but I can't. A lump develops in my throat. I look around the coffee shop to see who might be watching our little healing circle, but no one is paying any attention to us.

"Katie, you and I have been friends for a long time," Mariah says, holding the knife out in front of her. "I always...

admired and respected you. You were, like, so cool. Brainy, but not weird brainy, you know? You fit in everywhere. Then I watched as you became unraveled by a stupid game. You set up Joel and snubbed me for Warren. I couldn't believe you'd do those things. You didn't seem like the same person to me anymore, and now I don't know how to be with you." Mariah places the knife on the table, takes a ragged breath and wipes a tear off her cheek. Joel puts his arm around her shoulder and gives her a squeeze. She presses her face into his arm.

The lump in my throat has a stranglehold, but I pick up the knife and wait until I'm composed enough to speak. "First of all," I say, "I wish we'd done this in a more private place."

Joel and Mariah both smile a bit, and Mariah wipes away some more tears. "Too late now," Joel says. He rubs Mariah's arm. I wish it was mine.

I collect my thoughts and try swallowing the lump. "When I look back on that final night of the game, it's like looking into the hazy distance. Nothing is clear. You've got to know that I loved you both for being there for me, but at the same time, it was me that was suspended from school, and me that wasn't going to graduate if something didn't happen. And of course, things were even worse than you knew then. I'd lost the money, and I was…I was hurting real bad from what my dad had done to me."

I take a deep breath and let it out slowly. Then I close my eyes and continue. "When Warren called, I guess…

I guess I just fell apart and told him the truth. Not about my dad, but about losing the money, which I couldn't tell you about because I didn't want you to hate me. I didn't care what Warren thought of me. When he assured me that he'd make me win, I latched on to that promise. It was like a life ring, and I was drowning. I had nothing else. I figured you'd understand once the game was over, which was going to be that night anyway."

I feel hands clasp around mine, and I open my eyes. Mariah and Joel are both squeezing my hand, which is still clutching the stupid knife. I let the tears flow. "If you guys could have seen what they did to Warren, how they did it…"

I let go of the knife and drop my head to the table.

A moment later I feel a body slide into the booth beside me. A hand is rubbing my back. I look up and see Mariah there. She gives me a hug. Across the table, a throat clears. Joel is holding the knife again.

"If I'd known what you were going through with your dad," Joel says, "I…things would have been so different. And believe me, Katie, I would never have hated you for what you did." He shakes his head. "We do things for our parents. I'm sorry we haven't talked about this before…all that time wasted." He puts the knife down.

I reach for it one last time. "I couldn't talk about it."

He nods and picks up the knife again. He wipes his eyes with the back of his hand. "Katie, can we start again?"

"The healing circle?" I ask, horrified.

"No, silly. Us. You and me. And no Gotcha game."

Our eyes meet and hold, comfortably, for the first time all evening. I nod and smile and let Mariah rub my back.

As I slip into my new shoes and check my reflection in the mirror, I notice that I can still feel twinges in my ankle, especially with these heels, but the healing is almost complete. It's the night of the valedictory ceremony, and the robe will come off later. I'll be wearing my new dress under it, and even without Paige's help I think I've found one that suits me perfectly. It's ivory, with a halter top, a snug body and a hem cut in a jagged pattern. Mom helped me choose it, and I was surprised that she had such good taste. It didn't even cost a fortune.

After the formal part of the evening is over, a bunch of us are coming back here to celebrate. Mom has promised to stay in her room. I smile, thinking of our conversation this afternoon when I caught her making cookies for my party.

"Mom! We agreed. No more junk food in the house."

"But, Katie," she argued, "there is only healthy stuff in these. Cross my heart."

That's when I noticed the new blouse she was wearing. "More new clothes?" I ask.

"Yep, celebrating another five pounds gone. Forever."

"Way to go, Mom!" I try to give her a high five, but she grabs my arm and pulls me into an embrace.

I still find it awkward to hug her, but I'm trying. The morning after the Warren incident, after Fetterly left, we had a screaming match that probably echoed the fights she used to have with my dad. It started when she accused me of being weak, like him.

"What are you talking about?" I'd asked.

"That stupid game! You didn't have the courage to say, 'No, I'm not playing.' And then you gave your father the money when you knew damn well it was wrong."

"You're just as weak," I said, wanting to hurt her back.

"Really. How?"

"Just look at you."

She stared at me.

"You never go anywhere, do anything. You just make cookies and eat."

We screamed at each other some more before she stomped out of the living room, but I noticed she didn't go to the kitchen as usual. After pausing in the hall, she turned and went out the front door.

There was an icy silence between us for the next few days until, one night, she finally spoke. We were eating dinner, each of us with a section of the newspaper opened in front of us. It was the last day of my suspension, and the wall between us felt like a tower of cement. At some point during dinner I noticed she was no longer reading but staring at me. I glanced up.

"Katie, whatever happened to us?" she asked. Her eyes were welling with tears.

I was stunned. It's not like her to get all emotional with me. "What do you mean?"

"I mean…" She thought about it, choosing her words carefully. "When you were just a little girl…we had so much fun, right here at the kitchen table, creating stuff with play dough that we'd made from flour and food coloring, or…or we'd be in the sandbox, building castles. You'd putter along-side me in the garden, your hair a mass of ringlets around your head. You never stopped chattering, asking me questions about everything, from bugs to where babies come from."

I was sent spinning back to a time long forgotten. I saw her in that oversized apron she wore for gardening, with gaping pockets for her gloves and small gardening tools. In the spring I loved digging holes with a spade, and she'd gently place her seedlings in them. After carefully packing the soil around the delicate roots, I'd fill my small watering can and sprinkle the baby plants. All summer we watched them grow. We were a team.

Then Dad lost his job and Mom went back to work.

"I was mad at you for leaving me," I said, suddenly remembering the pain of being abandoned.

"Yes, you were." She nodded.

More memories came flooding back. How I hated waking up and finding only Dad home. He didn't under-stand that I wanted my egg soft and the toast cut in wedges so I could dip them in the mushy yolk. "Dippy eggs" Mom called them. And he wouldn't wait until my favorite TV show was over before we left the house to do chores or go on an excursion. He thought TV was bad for me. I hated him for that.

"You'd punish me when I got home," Mom said, her elbow on the table and her head resting in her hand. "You'd either throw a tantrum, kicking and hitting me, or you'd give me the silent treatment. I never knew what to expect."

I nodded, sitting back in my chair, trying to recall the turning point when Dad and I became pals and set up our own routines. Then Mom became the enemy.

"The other day you said that I never do *anything*," Mom said, changing the subject. "What is it you think I should be doing?"

I was embarrassed, thinking of that conversation, but I made some suggestions. "You know, walking, yoga, bike riding, Pilates." I thought of the things that Paige's mom was always doing. "You could take night classes. Maybe you could join a book club."

She thought about that. "Can you think of something we could do together?"

"Well," I considered it. "I've always wanted to try Tae Kwon Do."

She laughed. "Can you see me trying to kick anything? I'd fall over."

I laughed too. She was right. "Then why don't we start with yoga and see where we go from there."

She thought about that, and I saw a spark in her eyes for the first time in a long while. She looked...pretty. "It's a deal. I'll check into classes."

We sat in comfortable silence for a few moments, the cement tower a jumble of rocks and dust at our feet. I didn't understand what had just happened between us, but it was a relief, anyway. I felt like I was attached to a conveyor belt, and it was slowly but surely dragging me back up that water chute, bit by bit. Or maybe it was just a ladder that I had to climb, one rung at a time.

"Katie?"

"Yeah."

"I'm sorry I didn't talk to you about your dad. I...I just didn't know how."

I nodded. "I miss him."

She sighed. "I do too."

We stand in the hallway, in alphabetical order according to our last names, waiting to be marched into the theater for the valedictory ceremony. Everyone is chatting nervously. I get goose bumps just looking around at my fellow grads, some of whom I've known since kindergarten. It's hard to believe we're here, finally, wearing our matching robes and caps.

I spot Paige, about ten people ahead of me. We make eye contact but she quickly looks away. She agreed to come to one last grad council meeting with Warren and me, but she won't accept my apologies. I've come to accept that. I don't need someone so unforgiving in my life. I realize that it was my dad who brought us together in the first place in an attempt to help me overcome my shyness, and it's my dad's behavior that finally tore us apart. Maybe, left to our own devices, we wouldn't have been drawn to each other in the first place.

The band starts playing "Pomp and Circumstance," and now the goose bumps turn into a full-body rush as I follow the long parade of grads into the theater and to our seats on the stage. We rehearsed the whole thing this morning, but without an audience and the robes it had an altogether different feel.

There are speeches, and I watch as my classmates, one by one, march across the stage and shake Fetterly's hand. He hands them their diplomas, and various scholarships are awarded. As each person's name is called, their baby photo is flashed onto a large screen, which then melts into their formal grad photo. How far we've come.

Joel's name is called. As he walks across the stage, he makes eye contact with me and winks. I look up to see his baby photo. He was as cute then as he is now.

And then Warren's name is called. At first the applause is polite, restrained, but it gradually increases in intensity, becoming harder, more enthusiastic. I see Mariah, on my left, stand up to give him an ovation. One by one, more grads stand up. By the time he is shaking Fetterly's hand, at least half the grad class has risen to its feet. Only Warren could pull that off. He smiles and waves at us.

As I watch him pose for a photo with the principal, I remember the day I went to his house to talk about what had happened in the park. I started by apologizing for letting the mobbing go on so long.

"It wasn't your fault," he reminded me. "It was the Gotcha Gods."

I nodded and let it go.

Then I told him how hurt I was that he'd set me up. He shook his head and threw up his arms. "At what point did everyone forget that this was a game of strategy?" he asked.

I could only shrug. He was right.

"Are you sorry for anything?" I prompted.

He thought about that for a while. "I guess I'm sorry for some of the things I said to you that night," he admitted. "I was way out of line."

"I forgive you."

He looked surprised. Then he said, "Thanks for calling the cops. I hate to think of how far it might have gone. I was so friggin' cold!"

I could only laugh. "I'm just glad it was you that night, and not someone else."

"Huh?"

"No one else would bounce back so well. They'd be too mortified to go back to school, their egos crushed." I shook my head. "It must be nice to be so confident."

"Confident? Yeah, I guess." He actually looked surprised by that. "And I have a great body too, don't you think?" Warren smiled, that same old smile, and I knew he'd be okay. Better than okay. He'd be back on top in no time. I talked to him about my idea for the valedictory ceremony, and when I got ready to leave, he hugged me. It felt like the embrace of a good friend.

When my name is called, I'm handed my diploma and four scholarships, amounting to almost five thousand dollars. I look into the crowd, trying to find Mom's face. For a moment I think I see Dad's, but I'm mistaken.

After all the diplomas have been awarded, and the valedictorian has given her speech, it's time for grad council to do its thing. Part of it is expected, but part of it will be a surprise to the other grads. I'm nervous, wondering how they'll react.

We agreed to let Warren do the talking—after all, he has *that* voice. The seven of us approach the podium, and he waits until the theater is quiet before he begins. "As you know," he says, "it's a tradition at Slippery Rock High for the graduating class to honor the school with a gift. This year, those of us on grad council have decided to plant a young maple tree outside the front of the school. It is our hope that future generations of high school students can use it for shade on warm days and then enjoy the beauty of it in the fall, when its leaves turn to magnificent colors."

There's a polite show of approval, but it's really a most unremarkable grad gift, given what's been done in other years, and everyone knows that.

"As well this year," Warren says, "the graduating class is taking something away from the school." He pauses for dramatic effect. "We're retiring a long-held tradition, with hopes that the students of next year's graduating class will create something new, something fun and something safe."

Warren reaches into the hollow interior of the podium and pulls out the jar full of beads. He holds them up for everyone to see, and once again the glossy, multicolored beads slide across the smooth inner surface. "We're destroying the beads instead of passing them on to next year's class, as was the tradition. It's in this way that we feel we can make the most positive contribution to future generations of this school."

The theater is silent for a moment as people absorb what he has said. Then the clapping begins, and it turns into a thunderous roar. I can't see her, but I bet my mom is clapping loudest of all.

The after-party at my house was awesome. We laughed and cried and tried to imagine what we'd each be doing in ten years. Phillip recorded our predictions on video tape, and we planned to watch it at our ten-year high school reunion. We ate tons of junk food, and I sent the leftovers home with everyone so my mom wouldn't be tempted to cheat on her diet. Gotcha wasn't mentioned even once. I think that was intentional.

Joel was the last one to leave. He has completely forgiven me for betraying him in Gotcha. He helped me clean up, and then we chilled for a while. I felt…at peace. I didn't want the day to end, but we planned a hike for the weekend. It will be my first one since I last went with my dad years ago.

I'm too keyed up from the whole evening to go to bed. I turn on the computer and check my e-mail, an obsessive habit that I have to wean myself from. After all, it's been months since I've heard from Dad.

Tonight is no exception, but I'm feeling so mellow that I write him a note.

From: kittiekat17@hotmail.com
To: dannyo56@hotmail.com
Subject: I DID IT!

hey dad! i hope yur still checkin email.

guess what!!!! i gradded 2night,+ I got $5,000 in scholarships! whoo hoo!! i wish u could have been there. mom and i sure miss u.

xo
ur kittiekat

I shut off the computer and hope that wherever he is, he'll know that he's still loved. And forgiven. Well, maybe not completely, but I'm getting there. Joel has shown me the way.

Shelley Hrdlitschka is the author of a number of best-selling titles for teen readers, including *Sun Signs*, *Kat's Fall* and *Dancing Naked*. Shelley lives in North Vancouver, British Columbia.